Like a Bird

Becky Citra

**Library and Archives Canada Cataloguing in Publication**

Title: Like a bird / Becky Citra.
Names: Citra, Becky, author
Identifiers: Canadiana (print) 20240472411 | Canadiana (ebook) 2024047242X | ISBN 9781772604177 (softcover) | ISBN 9781772604184 (EPUB)
Subjects: LCGFT: Novels.
Classification: LCC PS8555.I87 L55 2025 | DDC jC813/.54—dc23


Cover illustration by Laura Atherton
Edited by Heather Tekavec

Printed and bound in Canada

*Second Story Press gratefully acknowledges the support of the Ontario Arts Council and the Canada Council for the Arts for our publishing program. We acknowledge the financial support of the Government of Canada through the Canada Book Fund.*

ONTARIO ARTS COUNCIL
CONSEIL DES ARTS DE L'ONTARIO
an Ontario government agency
un organisme du gouvernement de l'Ontario

Conseil des Arts du Canada
Canada Council for the Arts

Funded by the Government of Canada
Financé par le gouvernement du Canada
Canada



Published by
Second Story Press
20 Maud Street, Suite 401
Toronto, ON M5V 2M5
www.secondstorypress.ca

FSC
www.fsc.org
MIX
Paper | Supporting responsible forestry
FSC® C103567

# Like a Bird

BECKY CITRA

Second Story Press

*To Larry and Meghan, who are a huge part of this story*

## *100 MILE FREE PRESS*

### WILDFIRE THREAT LOOMS OVER BC

An exceptionally dry winter and persistent drought conditions have left soil parched and British Columbia's mountains with a snowpack of almost fifty percent below average. Currently, seventy holdover fires that smoldered through the winter in the northern regions of the province, with the potential to reignite in modern winds, are being monitored.

Government and wildfire officials are predicting a catastrophic fire season this summer and urge communities to put in place emergency plans. People using the backwoods are asked to use extreme caution.

# CHAPTER ONE

"For Christ's sake, slow down!" My grandfather Wayne jams his foot on an imaginary brake on the passenger side of his pickup. "Can't you see all those crows?"

I slam on the brakes.

Four glossy black crows are scrapping over a lump of brown fur in the middle of the highway. Red guts have spilled out onto the pavement, blood splattered in huge stars.

The crows scatter, straight up into the blue sky.

"Porcupine," says Wayne.

My little sister Jane's been reading in the backseat, her knobby knees pulled up to her chin. Now she's half out the open window. "Porcupine? Stop! Please, please, please, Rachel. Stop!"

I edge around the bloody carcass. "Put your seatbelt back on, Jane," I say. "Now!"

"I don't have any porcupine bones!" she says. "I've been dying for porcupine bones. Papa! Make Rachel stop! I need some porcupine bones for my collection!"

We're past.

The crows circle, waiting. I accelerate. Screeching, they plummet to the road. Jane thumps back against her seat.

Wayne turns around. "You can have an ice cream cone at the store."

Ice cream in early May makes me shiver, but Jane pops forward again. "How many scoops?"

Before Wayne can answer, I say, "One." I frown at her in the rear-view mirror. Her sugar consumption is out of control.

"Eyes on the road, girlie!" yells Wayne.

He takes his job as driving instructor very seriously. He's my designated driver. In other words, when I drive, he comes, too. Ever since the snow melted when I was still fifteen, he let me practice on the muddy, pothole-y logging road that goes to our ranch. Then I turned sixteen a few weeks ago, got my learner's permit, and today I'm on the highway. First time.

"Did you even see that car's turn signal?" he shouts.

"Jesus!" I swerve, barely miss skidding into the ditch, and then straighten the steering wheel. "Don't scare me like that!"

Jane jabs my shoulder. "I'm gonna barf!"

"Would everyone please be quiet," I say. "I am trying to concentrate."

~

When we get to the Aspen Lake store, Wayne stays in the truck. He has arthritis, and it's too painful for him to climb in and out. It's a chilly day, but I leave the front windows partly open.

Jane's ahead of me. She bounds up the front steps of the store and zips inside with a handful of coins from Wayne, straight to the ice cream counter. I pick up the mail from our box in the back corner, across from the coolers of soda and water, and flip through everything quickly. Letters from the Royal Bank, Ministry of Forests, our local MLA. A Save-on-Foods flyer. The John Deere tractor catalog. Wayne will never buy another tractor, that's over for him. But he'll also never cancel his catalog.

Two postcards all the way from the Black Sea in Turkey, one for me and one for Jane, from our counselor, Aura. We started seeing her after Mom died, when we were living in Vancouver with Uncle Rob and Aleksandra. Aura's traveling all over the world with her boyfriend, Mike. I used to get texts, but now she's trying to disconnect from her phone.

One more envelope. A white, legal-sized envelope with *Mr. Wayne Bird Box 33. Double D Ranch, Aspen Lake BC* on the front. It's my printing. An SASE. Self-addressed, stamped envelope.

I stare at it, my heart slowly accelerating, then fold it carefully and slide it into the back pocket of my jeans. I take the catalog and the rest of the mail out to the truck and pass it through the window to Wayne.

"That's all?" he says.

"Yup."

"Did you stick your hand right into the back of our box?"

"Yes, I did. I'm just going to say hi to Cody. And I'll get Jane."

Wayne grunts and flips open the catalog.

Jane's agonizing over ice cream flavors while Peggy, who's owned this store forever, waits patiently, the scoop in her hand. "How are your grandparents doing, Rachel?" she asks. "Margaret's well?"

People in Aspen Lake wonder about my grandmother. She's incredibly private.

"She's fine," I say. "They both are."

"Say hello from me."

Jane finally makes up her mind. "Bubble gum, please."

"Coming right up." Peggy nods at me. "Cody's in the back. Try not to distract him."

~

Cody's unpacking boxes of chips. I stand at the doorway and watch him. He looks good. He's wearing jeans and a sleeveless black T-shirt, and he's still got his suntan from skiing. He says his hair's getting too long, but I love it like this.

He glances up and smiles. He has such a great smile.

"Hey, Rach."

"Hey."

"Get over here."

We kiss quick, because there's always a chance that Peggy might come in. I pull back. "You're sweaty."

"Yeah, well, some of us have to work. What's up?"

"Picking up the mail. Wayne's in the truck. Jane's getting ice cream."

"Did you drive?"

"Yup. Piece of cake."

Cody and I have been going out for eight months and sixteen days. I talked to him for the first time at this very store. Second time we talked was the Aspen Lake rodeo. He'd cleaned up as the junior steer riding champion. I'd just moved here and had never heard of someone being a steer riding champion. I'd never even been to a rodeo before.

He wraps both arms around my waist. "Will you be pissed off if I don't come over tonight? Dad can't give me a ride, and it's gonna be too late to bike."

We'd planned to go out in my new canoe tonight. My birthday present from Wayne and Margaret. It's gorgeous, forest green lined with smooth, varnished wood the color of honey. A complete surprise.

"Uh, no…no, that's okay."

"You're sure?"

"I'm sure."

Cody lives with his dad, Jesse, and stepmom, Samantha, in a trailer on his grandparents' cattle ranch. It's nine miles, two on the highway and the rest on the logging road, between his place and mine. Definitely too far to bike after dark. He's had his learner's permit for almost a year, and by the end of next month, he'll be allowed to drive by himself. He's almost saved enough to buy a used pickup.

"Okay," he says. He kisses me again. "You got a ride to Sarah's tomorrow?"

"Tomorrow?"

"Yeah. We're playing Catan."

"I didn't know that. When?"

"Around three. Sarah probably thought you knew. Call me if Wayne or Margaret can't take you, and I'll ask Dad."

It's like that here. We're all so spread out. Our social life revolves around getting rides. Cody and I hang out with the same group, Dai, Tyson, Emma, and Sarah. They all went to Aspen Lake Elementary together. Then there's my best friend, Carlee. She's from Rocky Lake reserve, near the town of Hundred Mile. She has Rocky Lake friends, too, so she comes and goes.

It's not as perfect as it sounds. I'm only in the group because I'm Cody's girlfriend. He says that's bullshit, but it's true.

I walk back to the truck, analyzing what just happened. According to Aura, I overanalyze everything. This is where my brain's going: Is it bad to feel relieved that you're not going to hang out with your boyfriend on Saturday night? Is it bad to want to read a book instead? Did Cody even notice?

The thing is, I made a huge mistake last week, and I need some space to figure out what to do. So, I am relieved. And I'm not going to go to Sarah's. I don't believe that she thought I knew about it, and I don't think she cares if I come or not.

So. No date tonight. No Catan tomorrow.

Jane's standing beside Wayne's side of the truck. The top scoop of her ice cream toppled off and is now a bright pink puddle on the pavement. Wayne's digging around for more coins.

I'm losing the sugar battle.

~

The letter inside the SASE is short and to the point.

*Dear Mr. Bird,*

*Re: Query for:* A History of a Pioneering Family: The Birds, *by Wayne Bird.*

*We regret that this does not meet our needs.*

*Managing Editor*

*Peterson Press*

I flip open my laptop and go to my file called *Wayne's Book*. I find Peterson Press on my spreadsheet, type in today's date, and under the word *Reply*:

*Negative.*

Wayne spent years writing this book. I sacrificed my social life when I agreed to type it for him, and it's looking like he'll never get it published. I can't bear to tell him that. I crumple up the letter and the envelope and fire them into my wastebasket with all the others.

~

Margaret put a world map on a big bulletin board on the kitchen wall. Each time we get postcards, Jane marks the place with a colored pin. A line of them with colored heads winds through England, France, Spain, Italy, Greece, Croatia. Around the borders of the map, we're making a collage with all the postcards.

Jane finds Turkey on the map, then the Black Sea. She chooses an orange pin. Her postcard's of a beach with gorgeous turquoise water. Aura has scribbled *Guess what, Jane? The Black Sea isn't black!*

My postcard's of an ancient monastery clinging to the rock wall of a super high cliff. On the back: *Sümela Monastery. Insane if you have acrophobia!*

Then we play our game.

"Where would you go if you could go anywhere in the world tomorrow?" I ask.

"The pyramids in Egypt," says Jane. "Where would you go?"

I'd do what Aura's doing. I'd go everywhere. But I know where I'd go first.

"Paris," I say.

# CHAPTER TWO

The first time I rode my horse, Magic, alone last summer, I went to Butterfly Lake. That's where I'm going now. I've brought both dogs, our golden retriever, Bella, and our springer spaniel, Lucy. Lucy dives in and out of the bushes, following scents. Bella follows sedately. She's decided she's an elderly woman now.

Magic picks his way carefully along the deep ruts in the road. He's shedding his winter coat like crazy. A month ago, when I rode him, I put black rubber ice boots over his horseshoes so he wouldn't slip. Now, the ground's soggy in places, and we splash through dips in the ground filled with water. Deep in the shade, there's a tattered strip of old dirty snow. We come out at the ancient fir tree, at the top of the slope.

Below us, Butterfly Lake is a long narrow stretch of black mud with a narrow creek meandering down the middle. There used to be lots of water, before the old beaver dam broke and the lake drained. One day, beavers might come back and rebuild the dam. I hope so because it was beautiful. On a sunny day, the water shimmered like diamonds. It was Mom who named it Butterfly Lake.

I slide off Magic and hook the reins to the saddle, let him loose, and plunk down in the patchy shade under the fir tree. The creek is a silver trickle. Along the far side, dead trees stand like soldiers, white marks halfway up their trunks. That's how high the water used to be.

I'm always happy when I'm here but a little sad, too. My family has a dark side. A long time ago, there was a terrible car accident. Wayne, Margaret, and Uncle Jimmy were involved. Most of the time, I don't think about it. Except, sometimes, when I come here.

I'm wearing my down jacket, fleece-lined jeans, and earmuffs. Even though the sun's out, there's an icy wind. Spring takes ages to come to Aspen Lake because we're high up on a plateau. It's the tenth of May, and brown is still the dominant color. Bare brown branches on brown trees, last year's brown dead grass flattened by the snow, hollows in the ground filled with brownish snowmelt water.

But Wayne and Margaret say it's official. This is spring. Three weeks ago, the ice on Aspen Lake was mottled with dark gray patches and pools of surface water. Rotten ice. No one took the dogs anywhere near it. The ice crept away from the shore and, at the end of April, on a really windy day, all the ice sank. The sparkling water was back.

My first spring here. I gaze around. This is my place, like it was Mom's when she was sixteen.

My place. My horse. My canoe. A year ago, I didn't own anything important.

When I'm on the ranch, it does feel like my place. But to be honest, when I'm at school, not so much. I've got a boyfriend, I've got a best friend, but there are so many times when I feel like I'm on the edge of everything. That's the best way to describe it. Not left out, but not part of it, either. Like right now, everyone's playing Catan, and I'm here by myself. I know it's my choice, but it doesn't feel good.

They've been playing Catan for years, way before I got to Aspen Lake. They love it. You can have six players max, and I'm number seven. When I play, I team up with Cody or Carlee. I don't even like the game. I texted Cody last night and said Margaret needed me to watch Jane today. Not true. Jane's at her friend Cassie's.

And now I'm feeling shitty that I lied to Cody. And I'm wishing I was at Sarah's playing Catan, too.

A flash of white on the top of a tall, dead tree catches my eye. It's the bald eagle, the King of Butterfly Lake. He's enormous, and his snowy white head gleams. The King surveying his kingdom.

Where'd he come from? He hasn't been around since last summer. I made up this story that he was keeping our family safe. Then, when we didn't need him anymore, he left.

My spine feels prickly.

Why is he back?

~

I take a high school bus to the nearest town, One Hundred Mile House. I found out pretty fast that locals just say Hundred Mile, so I do, too. I get picked up and dropped back off at the Aspen Lake store. In the winter, I leave in the dark and come home in the dark. It was the same for Mom and Uncle Rob and Uncle Jimmy when they were kids. You get used to it. The pick up and drop off place for Jane's elementary school bus is at the pullout, halfway along the logging road.

This morning, we all sleep through the alarm. There's still time for Jane to make her bus, and Margaret dashes off with her, but my bus is long gone. I stay in bed, reading. It's Thursday, and what's interesting at school on Thursdays, anyway?

I read all morning. After lunch, Margaret works in her garden and Wayne disappears to write. I go back to my book. After a while, Margaret comes in and says she'll have a lie-down and to call her when it's time to pick up Jane. She's been doing that a lot lately.

That was two hours ago. I open her bedroom door a crack. She's in bed, asleep.

Wayne's bedroom is next to the laundry room, in a little hallway behind the kitchen. I bring him a cup of coffee. He's hunched over his desk, shuffling through a pile of loose papers. Bella's lying on his bed, her head resting on her front paws. She gives a low warning rumble in her throat.

This is a new and extremely annoying habit of Bella's. Wayne says she's being protective. I say she doesn't want anyone to make her do something she doesn't want to do. Like get off the bed and be a dog.

Her rumble turns into a proper growl. Wayne tosses her a dog treat from a tin on his desk.

"Oh, good. Reward her bad behavior." I set the mug down on the corner of his desk. "I brought you some coffee."

I glance around the cluttered room. Books everywhere—on his desk, in towers on the rug, crammed into bookshelves. Biographies of pioneers, books on raising cattle, histories of the world wars, books about Canadian explorers. I can't believe I spent two months in here typing his manuscript. He's started another book, this time about the history of cattle ranching in British Columbia.

"How's the new book coming?"

"Don't you have something else to do?" That's his writer's temperament. Cranky.

"Going to pick up Jane."

Wayne's too busy to notice that Margaret is still sleeping and that I'm heading out alone. Four miles of gravel road to the pullout, four miles back. Without my designated driver. It's against the law with just a learner's permit. But I want to know what it feels like to drive by myself.

~

There's been no rain, but the road's muddy from the melted snow. I splash around potholes. When I get to the junction, Susan, from the High Valley Ranch, which is just past our ranch, is waiting in her small blue car. We wave to each other as the bus rumbles up.

This road dead-ends at the High Valley Ranch, so Jane and Susan's granddaughter Cassie are the last two kids to get off the bus. They're in the same class. Best friends forever. They hop down, Jane first, then Cassie, giggling about something. Edna, the bus driver, taps her horn, makes a sloshy U-turn, and leaves.

I roll down my window. "Hey, Cassie."

"Hey, Rachel."

Jane climbs into the passenger seat then rolls down her window, too. "Goodbye, Cassie!" she yells.

Susan leaves first. Her car sprays mud, so I wait a few moments, then we head off.

I ease the truck over a part of the road that's like a washboard. Then I pick up speed.

"You're driving way faster than before," says Jane.

"I always drive—"

I swerve to miss a pothole, miscalculate, and we slide into the ditch.

*BANG!*

We lurch along, two tires in the ditch, two on the muddy road. A second, even louder *BANG* that might have been a big rock.

Jane screams.

I gun the engine. We bounce out of the ditch and back onto the road. There's a loud, grating, metal-scraping-ground kind of noise right beneath the truck.

"Is that us?" asks Jane.

"No. It's one of the other million trucks on this road."

"Does Papa know you're driving his truck all by yourself?"

The noise gets even louder. "Jesus." I pull over and turn off the engine. Jane scrambles out of the truck after me.

I squat down and peer underneath. I can't see anything hanging down, but then Jane calls out, "There's something falling off the back here."

It's the exhaust pipe.

"Is it supposed to touch the ground like that?" she asks.

I crouch and inspect the damage. "I can push it back up. If I just bend it—shit!" I stand up and blow on my hand.

"Is it hot?" says Jane.

I drive the rest of the way with my left hand, trying to ignore the metal-scraping noise, which is getting worse. Jane spins around so she can watch out the back window. "I'll tell you when it falls right off."

We make it home. Wayne's standing at the kitchen window, but his hearing is sketchy at the best of times. I'm safe. We go in through the mudroom.

Wayne thumps outside. A moment later, I can see him through the window, leaning over, staring at the exhaust pipe.

I'm banned from driving for a week.

# CHAPTER THREE

"Here's the deal," I say in the morning. "I fix the exhaust pipe, and you let me drive again. That's way more practical than banning me. You don't even like driving anymore."

Wayne frowns.

"Come on."

"It's got to be done properly," he says. "You can't stick it back with duct tape."

"Very funny."

"We need to do something," says Margaret. "I can't go into Hundred Mile with the truck making a noise like that."

"I'll fix it," I say. "How hard can it be?"

~

I watch several YouTube videos on fixing exhaust pipes. With fencing wire and Margaret's wire clippers, I lie on my back and use the bumper to pull myself under the truck. I couldn't see anything kneeling. I semi-close my eyes in case dirt or rust falls off and peer around.

The exhaust pipe disappears near the front of the truck. I'm only interested in the end that's dangling by my face. There's a clamp, broken into two pieces. One part is attached to the exhaust pipe, the other part is attached to something else.

I slide back out, cut a piece of wire, then slide back under. I squeeze the two pieces of broken clamp together and a shower of dirt rains down.

I blink hard, shut my eyes and mouth tight, bang against the exhaust pipe and the clamp, and wait until the rest of the dirt has finished falling. Then I start again. With one hand, I squeeze the clamp together. The exhaust pipe rises up like magic. With my other hand, I wrap wire around it. I cut another piece of wire and wrap that around, too, for good measure.

I stand up, dust off my jeans. Improvised, but quite spectacular.

~

I'm sitting with Carlee, Sarah, and Emma at a small table at the pizza place. They got here a few minutes before me and ordered a pepperoni and mushroom pizza. I'll have to pick off all the pepperoni because it's full of sodium.

Yesterday, Emma got her hair cut super short and dyed the color of dark chocolate. We've all been trying to adjust to her new look since the school bus this morning.

"Okay, opinions," she says. "Be honest. Does it look too weird with my eyebrows?"

Emma's eyebrows are the color her hair used to be, an almost white-blonde.

"No," we chime together.

"Where did you go?" says Carlee.

"Hairfinity."

We're impressed. Hairfinity opened a month ago, so Emma's our guinea pig. I'll need to know at least three people who have gone there before I'll risk it.

"They did a good job," says Sarah. "But your roots are going to be a major problem. When you grow it back."

That's a dig. Very Sarah.

"So, you're saying I should grow it back?" says Emma.

Sarah shrugs. "That's not what I said."

"It's original," says Carlee.

Emma looks suspicious. "Original good or original bad?"

"Original good," I say.

Sarah sighs. "Okay, we all agree that we like your hair, Emma. Now, where is our pizza?"

We pull out our phones. Sarah and Emma are on a mission to find the best cute cat YouTube video ever. Carlee looks up rodeo stuff. I text back and forth with Cody. He stayed home today because his mare Cheyenne is about to have her foal.

Carlee glances up. "What's Cheyenne doing now?"

"She's cranky. Pacing around. Peeing a lot."

"Good. That means she's ready."

The pizza arrives. I even hate the smell of pepperoni. I slip my phone in my pocket. "I'm going to go. I'm not even hungry. I'll see you back at school."

"Oh shit," says Carlee. "You don't eat pepperoni. Sorry."

"What's wrong with pepperoni?" says Emma. "Everyone loves pepperoni."

Cody says I sound very self-righteous when I talk about food. "Nothing's wrong with it," I say. "I'm just not that hungry."

This is going to look rude, but if I go now, I'll have enough time. "I'm going to take off. I'll see you later."

I stand and pick up my backpack.

"Rachel's going to the library," says Sarah in a singsong voice.

I analyze this all the way to the library. Is it the things that Sarah says...or the way she says them?

~

The library's in a huge log building on Birch Avenue. One of the librarians, Shanda, is behind the long counter at the front, taping the cover of a book. She's middle-aged, always smiling, and has a turquoise streak in her brown hair. She gets the record for reading more books than me.

"Hi there, Rachel."

"Hey, Shanda." I pile my return books in front of her.

"Any good ones?"

"Yeah, but nothing amazing."

"What's the word this week?"

"Blue."

I choose my books the same way Mom did. Today, I'm on a quest for books with blue in the title.

The library's quiet. A couple of women are on the computers, a man's reading a magazine in an armchair. I wander between the young adult and the adult shelves. Sun's slanting through big windows, and it's so warm in here you could almost believe the cold weather's gone forever.

I sit on the carpet and start the first chapter of *Into the Still Blue*.

The library fills with deafening noise. Little kids in jackets and boots, each clutching a picture book, pour in the front door. A harassed-looking woman is leading them, and a man is herding from behind. You only have to hang around Jane and Cassie for a day and you'd never want that job. I check the clock on the wall. 1:15. Uh-oh.

Shanda greets all the kids, then checks out my books, *Into the Still Blue* by Veronica Rossi, *Gathering Blue* by Lois Lowry, *Blue Lily, Lily Blue* by Maggie Stiefvater. And one more I've broken my rule for: *Lonely Planet: Pocket Paris*.

Shanda adds *The Bluest Eye* by Toni Morrison to my stack. "Not your usual pick, but I think you'll like it. See you next week, Rachel."

"Thanks, Shanda. See you."

I've had three lates already this week because I always have other, way more important stuff to do. But I take my time walking back, munching my apple. I'm not barging into the middle of math.

Today my word is blue. That's the mood I'm in. Don't ask me why.

~

"What are you doing?" yells Jane through the bathroom door.

"Washing my hair!"

"Can I come in?"

She's through the door without waiting for an answer. "What flavor is that?"

"Tropical pineapple." I hang my long, wet hair over the sink and turn on the blow-dryer. My hair is red. That's all you can say about it. The bathroom smells like Hawaii. Or how I imagine Hawaii smells.

Jane's taken the lid off the shampoo bottle and has her nose practically inside.

I turn off the blow-dryer and grab the bottle. "Breathing in chemicals will give you brain damage. I'm considering dying my hair. Follow the trend. What do you think?"

She wrinkles her nose. "Like Anne of Green Gables?"

I've read Jane the entire Avonlea series.

"Her hair turned green," she says.

"Good point," I say.

# CHAPTER FOUR

The colt is tiny, all long, gangly legs, knobby knees, wispy tail, and fuzzy mane. He's a rich chestnut, like Cheyenne, with his own unique white blaze on his face. Cheyenne's nibbling at a pile of hay in the middle of the corral while her colt skitters around. Cody and I are leaning against the top rail of the log fence. It's sunny but cold. I dig my hands into the pockets of my fleece jean jacket.

"What do you think?" says Cody.

"He's adorable. I can't believe he's walking already."

"He got up on his feet right after he was born." Cody sounds like a proud father.

"Thought of a name yet?" I ask.

"He's got his long-registered name, but I'm thinking Acorn. You like that?"

"Yeah, I do."

"We can go in and see him," he says.

We approach slowly. Cheyenne's mellow, rhythmically chewing mouthfuls of hay.

"Put your hand out," says Cody. "Let him come to you."

The tiny colt's eyes are huge, his ears pricked forward. When he walks toward me, his tiny ribs poke out. His velvety, soft dark muzzle nudges my palm. I stroke his neck gently.

"He's wonderful," I say softly.

"I know."

Cody rubs his hands over the colt's body, gently but firmly, down his neck, along his sides, under his belly, down his skinny legs. The colt bends his neck and mouths Cody's baseball cap.

"Okay, get outta here," he says.

The colt takes three hops and breaks into a jerky canter. Then he's back with Cheyenne, skinny legs splayed, reaching under her swollen belly for her teats.

We walk back to their trailer, a blue double wide. It's behind his grandparents' house, the old white farmhouse that everyone calls the Big House. His grandmother, Lois, is at her kitchen window, waving. We get along great, and I wave back.

I've figured out what I want to do," Cody says. "After I graduate. I want to breed and raise quarter horses."

That's new. "I thought you were going to raise cattle."

"That's what Grandpa wants me to do. But there's no future there."

"When did you change your mind?"

"I never made up my mind," he says.

I didn't realize he'd been thinking about this so much. Is he talking about right after graduation? That cuts out traveling together.

"What does Jesse say?"

"He wants me to do what I want to do."

Cody stops walking. He always does that when he's trying to explain something. I can walk and explain at the same time.

"I could build up a good business. Especially if we had a few more top mares like Cheyenne. I'll put some basic training on Acorn, and he'll be worth a lot of money when he's a two-year-old. Raising quarter horses would be my thing, not Grandpa's or Dad's."

"You'd need land." Practical me. "Where would you do this?"

The lights blink on in their trailer. That means Samantha's home. Jesse's in the barn, waiting for the vet to look at one of his new heifers. The huge hayfields beyond the buildings and corrals, sloping almost to the sky, are shadowy. Bands of clouds glow pink and purple.

"I'd do it here," says Cody.

Of course.

~

I'm riding with Amber today. She's Cassie's mom. They live at the High Valley Ranch with her parents, Susan and Martin. Amber grew up in Aspen Lake, and she was a really good friend of Mom's. And that makes her a special friend for me. I've just finished saddling Magic when she trots down our driveway on her big white gelding, Champion. We end up at Butterfly Lake. We sprawl out under the fir tree while Magic and Champion graze. We come here a lot.

Amber points to the dead tree. "Eagle."

I've never told her that he's the King of Butterfly Lake. That's something just for me and Jane.

It's peaceful today. There are changes even from last weekend. Blades of green grass are poking up through the old grass, and in the distance, a pale green veil is floating over the aspen trees. All the tiny new leaves, still curled up, ready to burst.

"How's Cody doing?" asks Amber.

"He's good."

"Okay." Her freckled face is turning pink. "I don't have a great track record with relationships, agreed?"

"Agreed." Amber is divorced. Between last November and this April, she had a boyfriend, a real estate agent like her. He was big time into video games, and he cheated on her. End of story.

"But I do have some experience," she says. "This is what I know: Guys think about sex all the time. They don't slow down until they're around a hundred."

I toss a pine cone at Magic's shoulder because he's moving too close. I definitely do not want to talk about this with Amber. Or anyone.

"Guys want sex," she persists.

I go still inside. Then I say, "You made your point. But Cody's not like that, if that's what you're getting at."

Amber snorts. "He's seventeen. He's exactly like that."

I'm starting to feel really uncomfortable. Amber wouldn't blab things I tell her, nothing like that, but she might let something slip out. She likes to talk.

"Do we need to have this conversation?" I say.

"No sex," she says. "Until you want to. Got it?"

"Got it."

I remember Mom cornering me one night after Jane had gone to bed. I was fourteen. "We need to talk," she said.

"About?" I said.

"About boys."

Problem was, Mom's experiences with men were mostly bad. It was hard not to come away thinking all guys were losers.

Amber's freckles go even darker when she's giving me advice.

"And you use birth control. But before that, you talk to me."

~

Cody and I had sex two Saturdays ago. Jesse and Samantha went to Hundred Mile to meet some friends at the new Italian restaurant. We started out on the couch, watching a movie on Netflix and eating popcorn. We ended up in Cody's bed.

That's the huge mistake I made.

We weren't totally irresponsible. We used a condom. But something went wrong. Cody was fumbling around and he said, "Shit!" and now I'm terrified that I might have gotten pregnant. My period's not due for another week. That seems like forever away. Then I'll know for sure.

It wasn't like we'd never done anything before. We'd come close to sleeping together, but we always stopped. Cody said he'd buy some condoms. One day. We hadn't planned to go all the way that night. God.

It was Cody's first time, too. He kept asking me if I was okay and he said any time I changed my mind, it would be okay with him. It was nothing like I'd imagined. I guess I thought the first time would be this special magical moment, but it wasn't. That physically everything would be smooth and effortless and time would stand still. It didn't. That I would feel different, more confident, but I feel exactly the way I always have.

That's not true. I do feel different. But not in a good way.

It was over so fast. It was awkward. It hurt a bit and was kind of messy. But at just the right moment, I opened my eyes and Cody gave me one of his huge smiles. I loved being so physically close to him.

When Jesse drove me home, Cody and I sat in the backseat, holding hands. We kissed too, just once, quickly. I was terrified Jesse would know. It was so obvious. But Cody leaned forward, and he and Jesse just chatted about regular stuff. Horses. The rodeo. Cody sounded just the same. What does that say about what happened? That it wasn't that big a deal to him? The whole way I said just one thing to Jesse, something about Wayne, and my voice sounded totally weird, like I was a robot or something.

Most of the time, I just sat there, staring out the window. I was a frozen ball of...guilt?

~

Cody and I agreed on two things:

He won't put pressure on me to do it again.

We won't do it again until I go on the pill.

But I do feel pressured. And I'm not going to go on the pill. I don't want to have sex again. It didn't make me feel good, and it changed everything. Before, I wanted to be with Cody all the time. Now I don't know what I want. It's not Cody's fault. It's me.

# CHAPTER FIVE

Margaret, Wayne, and I are having coffee on the verandah.

"Martin's putting his cows out this week," says Wayne. "We need to make sure all our fences are still up."

It's Margaret who looks after the fences now. Wayne can't because of his arthritis. Martin and Susan have a permit to put their cows out on free-range from the middle of May to October. That means the cows can wander around all summer, grazing in the forest and meadows and along the sides of the road. It's our responsibility to keep them out of our ranch.

"There's a rancher down in Barriere who got a permit somewhere up here, as well," Wayne grumbles on. "Cows getting in. Christ, that's all we need."

We used to be a cattle ranch, too, but it got too much for Margaret and Wayne. They sold their cows, and Martin leases the hayfields. Nobody wants cows in here now, trampling the hay and making trouble. Martin helps us with the fences when he can, but there's always a million things to do at the High Valley Ranch. Margaret rides along our fence line every week, looking for trees that have fallen on the wire or posts knocked over by animals. I help out, too.

She seems miles away, but she sets her coffee mug down. "There's that one stretch of fence we left last week. We said we'd do it next time, Rachel. Remember?"

It was two weeks ago when we left that section of fence. Not one week. I know because that was the weekend I was pulling an all-nighter finishing a history project. I don't think Margaret's ever left the fences for two weeks.

Why didn't I think about the fences?

"I'll go," I say.

"By yourself?"

"Yeah. I do know what to do, you know."

Margaret massages the base of her neck, a sure sign she's getting a migraine. "I know. But Cody's coming over, isn't he?"

"Not till later."

"Don't try and check the whole fence line. Just the part in the trees on the other side of the lower hayfield. Okay?"

"Got it."

"Leave the dogs here," says Wayne. "And pay attention out there."

Because of bears? Because I'm riding by myself? He doesn't say.

~

I find one place where the post has been yanked right out of the ground. It's one of the old posts, half rotten. Margaret has shown me all the places where Uncle Jimmy put in new posts. He was going to replace all the rotten ones. He died before he finished.

I'm in a low spot. It was really swampy a couple of weeks ago, but it's starting to dry up. The wire sags, and the top strand has snapped in half. A tuft of black fur is caught on a jagged barb. Bear. I jump down off Magic and hook his reins to the saddle. Then I take my leather work gloves, a roll of wire, and fencing pliers out of my saddlebag.

Margaret's way better at this than me. I hunt around for a long, thick branch. When I find one that looks strong enough, I weave it through the fence wires, propping everything up again. It's makeshift, but so is everything on our ranch now.

I twist each end of the broken wire into a loop. This is the trickiest part. I take a piece of wire and join the ends, yanking everything tight with the pliers. I raise my shoulder to chase away a mosquito. First mosquito of the year. The pliers slip. The wire ends spring apart and a barb stabs my finger. I suck the blood, then start again.

Finally, I step back, swatting more mosquitoes away from my face. It's not a great job, but I think it will work. I get back on Magic and follow the fence, mostly through forest. I find one more place where two posts are leaning over, but nothing is broken. I prop the fence up, weaving sticks through the strands of wire.

I walk from there to the corner where two fences meet, leading Magic. Everything looks good here. I haven't really done all that much today, but I feel like I've accomplished something.

I'm in no hurry to get back. Magic and I leave the fence and follow a trail through a maze of fallen trees, the trunks black. Pine beetle kill. One of the first effects of climate change? It was a long time ago, but everyone in Aspen Lake still talks about it. My legs hang softly, putting no pressure on Magic to walk faster. His neck is slick with sweat. I lean forward and stroke him. His long black ears swivel around.

We come out in a meadow and ride to the end where there's a steep, grassy hill. We climb to the top. I get off and let Magic graze. You can see so much from up here—the lake, our fields, the dark green metal roof of our log house, the marsh, and the old homestead, built by my great-great-grandfather.

Margaret brought Jane and me up here on our first week last summer. City girls, straight out of Vancouver. We'd never been to Aspen Lake, never met Wayne and Margaret. Before Mom died, we didn't even know we had grandparents. When we were living with Uncle Rob, he used to make the six-hour drive to Aspen Lake all the time, but he never took me and Jane. I was expecting Aspen Lake to be a little town, but it's not. Just a general store across the road from the lake, a gas station, and the elementary school. And I'd had no idea what it would be like to live on a ranch.

I think Margaret wanted us to really understand where we were. Even more important, what we were becoming part of.

Jane dragged a smelly deer carcass out of the bush. It was the beginning of her bone collection.

It was the beginning of everything.

# CHAPTER SIX

"Can I play?" says Jane. "Please, please, please."

"No," says Cody.

"Yes," I say.

I don't miss the look on Cody's face as Jane plunks down at the kitchen table. "Don't you have to pack your stuff?" he says.

We've been killing time playing blackjack until Susan gets here to pick up Jane for an overnight with Cassie. As soon as Jane's gone, we're paddling out to the island. Margaret's lying down and Wayne's watching TV, and right now someone has to keep an eye on Jane.

"I'm already packed," she says.

I jump in with "We'll play Crazy Eights," because it's fast and she knows how to play it.

Cody thinks I spend too much time with Jane. It's one of the things we fight about.

He deals the cards, *slap, slap, slap*. He calls this babysitting, as in *Do we have to babysit Jane again?* I think of it more as hanging out with my little sister, like I've always done. But Cody doesn't have brothers or sisters so he doesn't really get it.

"Two games and then you have to find something else to do, okay?" I say to Jane.

Jane's on a winning streak, smashing her cards on the table. Cody looks bored. Me? I'm ten percent here, ninety percent somewhere else. This morning, I was sure I felt a twinge in my gut that felt like cramps, which was weird because my period isn't due for three days, and I'm never early. I prayed it was the beginning of my period, and I kept checking and double checking the calendar, hoping I had miscalculated, but I hadn't. Then the cramps went away, anyway.

This is so freaking stressful.

Outside the kitchen window, a car honks. A minute later, Cassie bursts into the kitchen. Her face, as freckled as Amber's, is pink.

"Hey, Rachel!" she says.

"Hey, Cassie."

She stares at Cody. She's a little in awe of him. Jane races upstairs and comes back with her overnight bag. She gives me a very long hug because she always feels homesick when she goes somewhere, even before she leaves.

"I'm going now," she says.

"Finally," says Cody.

Jane sticks out her tongue.

~

After Butterfly Lake, the island is my favorite place. It's tiny, with tall fir trees and only one good place to land, between two big rocks. It's a fifteen-minute paddle from the shore, the last few minutes through lily pads that rustle against the bottom of the canoe.

The lake is glass and the sun is warm, but the water's still too cold to swim. I'm lying on my stomach on a towel spread out on the grass, wearing my blue bikini. I don't tan. I burn. That goes with my red hair. But I never give up trying. It's my mission in life.

Cody's hunched over, snapping a dry stick into little pieces. Then I feel him trace his finger right down my spine. I wiggle because it tickles. The bikini was a mistake. I should've at least kept my T-shirt on.

I roll over and sit up.

"What's wrong?" he says.

"Nothing." Since we had sex, I don't want Cody touching me like that. I tense up inside. I try not to, but I can't help it.

"Okay, nothing's wrong." He digs in the side pocket of his baggy shorts, pulls out a small white box.

My heart slams to a stop.

He hands me the box. I open it. Inside, resting on a square of cotton batten, is a ring. A green stone set in a plain silver band. I pick it up. It's small in my palm, and it feels like it should be heavier.

"It's not an engagement ring," he says quickly. "Obviously."

"God, I hope not." I give a little barky laugh. "So...it's a *non*-engagement ring," I say. "A promise ring."

"Right."

That means—what? We care about each other. We're committed to each other. We're not going to go out with anyone else. I'm okay with that, I really am, but this doesn't feel good. I don't know why. Couldn't he have just given me a necklace?

Cody's clearly waiting for me to say something else. I can hear him waiting. I could try, *Shouldn't we have discussed this first?*

I've been quiet for too long. He's not talking either. Loons are warbling in the dark shadows along the far lakeshore. The sun's going to sink behind the ridge any minute.

I'm still staring at the ring. Finally, he says, "It's an emerald… your birthstone and…is something wrong? And don't say nothing again."

"We said no pressure."

"This isn't pressure. What? You think I'm giving you a ring so you'll sleep with me? Come on, Rachel."

I look at his face. Tanned, and his shaggy hair is so long, and his eyes are green like the emerald. I'm scared I'm going to cry.

He blows out air. "Well, that went well."

But there's that little crease between his eyebrows that always means he's upset. "I'm sorry. It's just…. Shit, Cody. I wasn't expecting this."

"Are you gonna try it on?"

"Yeah…of course." I lift the ring off its fluffy cushion, slip it on my finger. It fits perfectly. Of course it does. Cody never screws up.

We both stare at it. It's very sparkly.

"It's beautiful," I say.

He pulls me toward him. "I love you."

"I love you, too."

"Are you sure?"

"Yes, I'm sure."

We have this conversation a lot lately.

His "Are you sure?" is a blip in his confidence that you hardly ever see.

He pushes my long hair away from my face and kisses me. It's a long kiss. I love kissing Cody…but not right now.

He pulls away. "Keep the ring, for a while, anyway. You don't have to wear it if you don't want to."

He's giving me permission?

"I don't know if I—"

"Keep it. Until I think of someone else to give it to."

"Ha-ha."

I shouldn't accept the ring. I know that. I'm sinking deeper and deeper into...what? What is it exactly that Cody and I have? I also know that I'm getting overwhelmed, and when I get overwhelmed, I have a bad habit of doing the opposite of what I want to do.

I put the ring back in the box. I pull on my T-shirt and shorts and push the box deep into my pocket. The ring can't fall into the lake. That would be very bad.

We paddle back in silence. Sometimes, when the sun goes down, the sky and the lake melt into molten copper. It doesn't always happen, and it doesn't happen tonight. Everything just gets dark purple blue, almost black. The loons are quiet now.

This is what a non-engagement ring says:

Rachel is Cody's girlfriend. One day they'll get engaged. And then married. And then they'll have babies.

Okay, I'm exaggerating. And you don't have to do it like that anymore. You can have a baby whenever you want to. No one cares. Except me.

~

How can your skin stretch that much? Does your stomach ever look normal again?

I do know one thing. Your hormones go crazy. And you get weird cravings for pickles, and your feet swell up like balloons, and you're always exhausted. You get major skin breakouts. And then you start feeling the baby kicking. And then labor. God.

And then what do you do? You have to figure out how to look after a whole other tiny person when you're still trying to figure out how to look after yourself.

I roll over on my bed, press my face into my pillow, and burst into tears.

# CHAPTER SEVEN

"I already know about the ring," says Carlee.

"You do?"

"Yeah."

"He *told* you?" I really hate Carlee knowing before me. Most of our hanging out is at school because she lives so far away. We text all the time. When it's major news, we phone. Right now, I'm on the landline in the kitchen because our cell service is bad.

"What are you going to do?" she asks.

"I'm not going to wear it, if that's what you mean."

Silence. What did I expect? Carlee's dead loyal to Cody. They've been competing in rodeos together for hundreds of years before I got here. Cody rides steers, Carlee barrel races. They cheer each other on. Their bond is special, different from what I have with either of them.

"Why not?" she says finally.

"Because he didn't ask me first. Because I don't want to."

"Is it because—?"

I've told Carlee about having sex. The whole story. I can trust her one hundred percent not to tell anyone else.

"No."

"Rachel."

"It's not."

"You're sure?" she says.

"Yes."

"Okay," she says. "What did you say to him?"

"I don't know. I don't remember exactly." Is that icy voice mine? "And in the future, I would appreciate it if you and Cody didn't plan things behind my back."

"We didn't plan anything," she says. "I just said I knew."

"Well don't even talk about me with Cody. This is between me and him."

"Okay. Then why did you bring it up?"

Carlee always sounds so logical when she's being illogical. "Because you're supposed to be my friend? Because you're clearly more Cody's friend than mine?"

Where did that come from? Is it even true? No. I'm just feeling crappy.

"That's ridiculous," she says.

"Carlee, do you think just once you could support me instead of criticizing me?"

"I do. All the time."

"If you say so. Let's change the subject."

I stare at Aura's postcards. I'd give anything to be in one of those places right now. I don't care where. Just anywhere that's not Aspen Lake.

"Rachel, sometimes you're so—" Carlee stops.

"I'm so what?"

"Nothing."

"No. Sometimes I'm so what?"

"Okay, but don't get pissed off. It's just that lately, sometimes... you can be very self-absorbed."

~

Carlee calls me back.

"I'm sorry. Self-absorbed was the wrong word."

What was the right word? "That's okay."

"I didn't mean it."

"It's alright."

"I didn't actually mean anything. I know you've been really stressed about Cody. So...truce?"

"Truce. And I didn't mean what I said either."

"When is your period due?" she asks.

"Tuesday. Why? What are you thinking?"

"Just wondering when you'll start acting normal again."

~

I can see Margaret's floppy hat over the top of the weathered, gray garden fence. She's sitting on a chair with a big, curved back, made of bent willow sticks. There's another chair just like it on the verandah. Once, Jane was sitting in it and tilting it backward and Wayne said, "Don't break Jimmy's chair!"

"Did Uncle Jimmy used to sit here?" said Jane.

"Uncle Jimmy made that chair," said Wayne.

He must have made the chair in the garden, too. I didn't know that before. So much I didn't know about Uncle Jimmy. Jane and I never got to meet him.

Margaret's garden is like a secret garden. In the summer, vegetables and flowers are mixed together in a mass of color. In May, it's still just a promise that things will grow. The delphiniums are green mounds, the roses and the raspberry canes still don't have leaves, and stiff daffodils are pushing through the soil. The raised vegetable beds are bare dirt except for tiny lettuces and spinach plants and a long row of peas reaching for their trellis.

"Hello there, Rachel," she says when I get closer.

"Can I do anything to help? Weeding or watering?"

"No, I don't think so. But that's very sweet of you." She stands up. "You could help me cover the garden. It's clear out, so there'll be a frost tonight."

In Aspen Lake, the temperature can plummet twenty degrees in a few hours. Margaret's really good at predicting frost. It can be hovering just above zero, and Wayne will say, "You'd better cover," and she'll say, "Oh, I don't think so." Other times, she's covering plants when we're in bathing suits. She's never wrong.

I help her pop a plastic hat called a cloche over each tiny bean plant. Then we drape big white cloths that look like sheets over all the raised beds.

"Thank you, Rachel," says Margaret. "I'm going to stay out a little longer. You go in."

I stop at the gate, not wanting to leave but not knowing why. A tiny brown, speckly bird flits about in the raspberry canes. Margaret's sitting again, her head tilted back, eyes closed. Is she remembering when Uncle Jimmy built her chair?

I have this sudden overwhelming urge to tell her everything. It would be such a relief. Margaret always knows what to do. But I don't tell her. She's obviously tired. She doesn't need my drama.

~

Jane's still at Cassie's. I join Wayne and Margaret in the living room where the news is on. We watch a mountainside burn up.

Fires have names. This is the Eagle Bluff fire. One thousand acres have burned. They've sent in twelve firefighters and one helicopter.

"Twelve firefighters doesn't sound like a lot," I say.

The TV screen switches to somewhere called Saddle Creek. A fire is sweeping closer and closer to a subdivision. Human-caused. "I think that's where Tom and Karen Williams moved," says Margaret.

"Who?" Wayne's picking burs out of Bella's ears and dropping them on the carpet.

"Remember? Jimmy's soccer coach? They bought a very expensive home somewhere in there. They must be frantic."

Margaret was knitting, but she's put her needles down.

"They should close the backcountry," says Wayne. "Keep out all the goddamn joyriders from the coast with their goddamn ATVs."

"We're so lucky to live way up on the plateau," says Margaret. "Removed from it all. It's always so much hotter and drier down in the valleys."

"Not always," says Wayne.

The screen jumps to a woman with a microphone, her long hair blowing back from her face, a smoky hillside behind her.

"I'm reporting to you from Slack Lake," she says.

"Hm?" says Margaret. "I've never heard of Slack Lake. Have you, Wayne?"

Wayne leans forward, closer to the TV. "It's down the Big Hill," he says.

The Big Hill starts at a place called Little Fort and climbs steadily to Aspen Lake. The temperature drops with every mile you climb. It can be raining in Little Fort and snowing in Aspen Lake. Unless you're in the middle of a heat wave, and then it's hot everywhere.

"The fire started late this afternoon," says the woman. "A local resident claims it was caused by a dropped cigarette. Conditions here are exceptionally dry, however, the wind conditions are favorable. Firefighters expect to have it contained shortly."

"Slack Lake must be as small as Aspen Lake," says Margaret. "Not a lot of houses, I imagine. A cigarette. Especially now when everything's getting so dry. People don't think."

"It's on the other side of the Thompson River. Thank God for that." Wayne stands up. "It's time for our walk, Margaret."

~

Margaret and Wayne walk every day before bed, up the driveway.

"If I don't use my goddamn legs, I'll lose them," he always says.

They walk for about twenty minutes, as far as a tall, leaning pine tree that one day will fall and tear down our power line. Wayne won't consider cutting it down to avoid this impending disaster (no power line, no internet). It's an old tree that defied the pine beetles. It deserves to stand as long as it can.

Wayne pushes himself ahead with his canes. Sometimes, his legs work well and he hobbles along. Sometimes, he just stabs the air with the canes or they skitter sideways on the gravel. The pine tree is the goal. Wayne's marker. His proof that he can still do it. He'll get there even if it kills him.

Margaret walks slowly beside him.

When they get back, Margaret makes them both a mug of warm malty Ovaltine. Jane calls it the Old People's Drink.

~

Monday is Queen Victoria's birthday, but only people like Wayne and Margaret call it Victoria Day. For the rest of us, it's the May long weekend. No school.

Margaret, Jane, and I go for a ride together, me on Magic, Margaret on her gelding Dancer, and Jane on her little black and white pony Dixie.

The world has turned green. It's such a surprising green, not like you see in Vancouver where it's never *not* green. Here, it changed almost overnight, from brown to a haze of pale green over the aspens to this explosion of intense green. It's almost fluorescent in the sun. The sky is blue, cloudless. The horses have spring fever, and we give them little checks with the reins to keep them from jogging. It's a short ride, just down through the fields to check a fence.

It hasn't rained for two weeks. That never happens here in May, except this year. It's seventy-nine degrees Fahrenheit. That also never happens in May.

"They're predicting a very hot June," says Margaret. "Lots of forest fires. I thought it was hot last summer, but this is shaping up to be worse." Birds are singing everywhere. It's mating season. "You wait," she says. "In a few weeks you won't hear a sound. They'll all be in their nests."

Margaret and Wayne don't need a calendar. They know what date it is just by looking and listening. I'd love to be able to do that, too.

"A bone!" shouts Jane.

I hold Dixie's reins while she slides to the ground. She pulls something long and grayish-white out of a clump of bushes. Margaret and I have rules: No attached flesh, rotten or fresh. It can't stink.

Jane's bone passes the test. Margaret ties it to her saddle. It's some kind of leg bone. Or a rib.

Wayne will know.

# CHAPTER EIGHT

"My period's late," I say.

"By one day, Rachel," says Carlee. "That's nothing."

We're at the lockers, just before our last class. For once, the hallway is deserted. I've been waiting all day to get Carlee alone.

"Not if you're me, it's not," I say. "I'm never late."

Except once. After Mom died, I didn't get my period for two months. That made sense, my world had just collapsed. But it's never happened since. I'm Ms. Regular. I'm like a clock.

"And look at my skin," I say.

"Your skin looks fine."

"I know. But I always get a few pimples right before I get my period. So, what does that mean?"

"Search me." Carlee lowers her voice because two Grade Nine girls have just come out of the art room door carrying a paper-mache project on a board. "But you said you used a condom."

"Shhhh." When the girls have gone, I say, "We did."

"Was it a good quality condom?" says Carlee.

"How am I supposed to know that?"

We laugh. Carlee, that little spurt that comes out of her nose. Me, hysterically. I close my eyes for a second.

"This isn't funny, Carlee," I say.

"Did it break?"

"No. I don't know. Maybe it did."

"They can leak," she says. "Sometimes.... Well, that's probably rare."

"That makes me feel way better."

"Have you told Cody?"

"No," I say. "And don't you dare tell him yourself."

"Is that the kind of friend you think I am?" she says. "Thanks, Rachel."

"Sorry."

"Personally," she says, "I wouldn't panic yet."

"This is my punishment for keeping the ring," I moan.

Carlee glances around. "We better get to class."

It's math, and we're reviewing for a test, but I say, "I'm getting out of here."

Carlee frowns. She takes authority way too seriously. She gives me a big hug. "Don't worry. We'll figure it out. I'll see you later."

I'm trying not to feel abandoned by my best friend. When I get to the front door, she pops up. "We need to get a home pregnancy test."

~

"Shit, it's Wednesday."

Carlee and I have crossed the highway, and we're walking to the drugstore on Birch Avenue.

"Right," says Carlee. "The day after you were supposed to get your period. And that means…?"

"Margaret's shopping day. I completely forgot. She thinks I skip too many classes. I'll be grounded."

"She won't see us," says Carlee. "Town's always crazy busy on Wednesday."

"Eagle eye Jane's with her."

"Not good."

We stick to the shady side of the street, hanging back under the awnings and checking the line of parked vehicles for our pickup. I stay by the drugstore door while Carlee does a quick recce inside.

"Coast is clear," she says.

I grab a wire basket, then we separate and glide up and down the aisles. I'm not sure what Carlee's doing, but I'm pretending to look for something else while I look for the pregnancy test. I fill the basket with miscellaneous stuff that I don't need so, when I get to the till, I can bury the pregnancy test in toothpaste, dental floss, hair conditioner, moisturizing cream, etc. In case I see someone I know.

The same aisle as the pads is a possibility. Nope. And why is Carlee in the baby section? I find the condoms. Who knew there were so many different brands? Is this where Cody bought them? What kind did he buy? And when exactly did he buy them? Why didn't he tell me?

Maybe he used Jesse's? My head is exploding. I've lost my focus. Where are the stupid pregnancy tests?

"Found them!" whispers Carlee from the end of an aisle.

They're next to the lubricants.

A stack of pink rectangular boxes.

*First Response Pregnancy. No other brand tells you sooner. 6 Days sooner. Easy-to-read results. Over 99% accurate.*

Too much information. My legs are shaking. "You're right," I say. "Why am I panicking?"

I ditch the pregnancy kit and the basket of other stuff, and we flee. We stand outside the drugstore, convulsed in nervous giggles, and our truck goes by, Jane's face staring at us through the side window.

~

Margaret picks me up at school.

Teaching me to drive is Wayne's job, not Margaret's. I slide in the front passenger seat. Jane's behind me. The back of the truck is filled with grocery bags and electric fans.

Jane leans forward and whispers in my ear, "You're in big trouble."

I ignore her. "What's with all the fans?"

"The Farmer's Almanac is predicting a heat wave next month," says Margaret. "I was afraid they'd sell out."

She turns onto the highway. "How was school today?"

"Good."

No more questions. But I'm still on guard.

"Hey," says Jane. "Can I get an ice cream cone?"

"I don't appreciate being called 'Hey,'" says Margaret.

"Can I get an ice cream cone, Nana? Please, please, please."

"No," she says. "We've been in town long enough. And there's ice cream at home."

"It's vanilla," says Jane.

"What's the matter with vanilla?"

"I *despise* vanilla."

I can see Margaret's hands tighten on the steering wheel.

"Fine!" Jane kicks her feet hard against the back of my seat.

"Oooof!" I say.

Margaret veers over to the shoulder on the side of the highway, stops the truck, turns off the ignition. "You can just get out and walk, young lady!"

Jane is too stunned to do anything. Me too. Cars are flying past us. This feels dangerous.

"Or do you want to be a grateful little girl and get a ride?"

"Get a ride," whispers Jane.

"Alright," says Margaret. She puts on the turn signal and eases out into the traffic. On the way home, no one talks. Margaret's in a lousy mood. So what? It doesn't mean that it's like last year, after we moved here. Because of all that bad stuff that had happened in the past, Uncle Rob said that there would be gossip and that it would be hard. He was worrying about me and Jane starting new schools in the middle of it all, and he was worrying about Wayne who had just had a heart attack.

No one was worrying about Margaret. She kept on going, making dinners, doing laundry, nursing Wayne. We should have worried about her, and then it was too late. In October, she had a kind of nervous breakdown and ended up in the hospital for ten days.

I never ever want that to happen again.

We make a quick stop at the Aspen Lake store. Jane's zonked out, her cheek pressed against her window. I dash inside the store and check our mailbox. Another SASE with my handwriting on the front.

When we get to our road, I get out and open the gate. Wayne's first KEEP OUT sign is still nailed on the post. There are two more signs, TRESPASSERS WILL BE PROSECUTED and KEEP OUT, on trees along the two-mile driveway to our house. They're tipping sideways, hanging on by loose nails. One last sign, NO TRESPASSING, has fallen into the grass. That's okay. We don't need these signs anymore.

~

*Dear author,*

*Re:* A History of a Pioneering Family: The Birds *by Wayne Bird.*

*Mooncrystal Books publishes exclusively new age books focusing on meditation and personal development. We also have a small line of vegan cookbooks.*

*In the future, I strongly advise you to research a publisher's backlist before submitting your manuscript.*

*Editor*

*Mooncrystal Books*

~

I'm grounded.

"You know how Wayne and I feel about you skipping classes." But Margaret's heart is not in this. Even when I skip, I get really good marks. "Just for the weekend. And you can still work at the bookstore on Friday. And you can ride if you want."

"Okay."

The bookstore's the most important thing. It's called Wagonroad Books, and I work there every Friday after school. I can't miss that. Saturday, there's a party at Emma's dad's place. There'll be other kids there, too, not just our group. Emma lives one week with her dad and one week with her mom. Her dad lets us have coolers, sometimes even beer. That started after Christmas. I liked it better before because the guys can act so stupid when they drink. I don't mean Cody. He's not interested in drinking. Me neither. Long story short, I don't care if I miss Emma's party.

We put the groceries away in an easy silence. Margaret's not mad, just tired. I'm glad I'm grounded. It gives me an excuse not to go to the party.

I text Cody.

Me: Margaret caught me skipping I'm grounded for the weekend
Cody: I wanted to see you
Me: Me too

Not true. Right now, it's easier to be by myself.

# CHAPTER NINE

I love the smell of our barn, especially in the early morning. It's a mix of hay and grain and leather. Signs with the names of horses burned into the wood hang above the eight stalls. Margaret's the horse person in the family, and she often talks about all the horses they used to have. Now we're down to three. Winter's over, and Magic and Dancer and Dixie won't use their stalls again until the fall.

I scoop grain from a barrel into three shallow, black rubber tubs. Carrying them out to the field, I whistle. Hooves pound, each horse blowing through his nostrils, jostling for his place. Then it's down to serious eating. I go back to the barn and get three flakes of hay.

Another few weeks and they'll be munching on green grass up to their bellies. They won't need me until the fall, either. I'll miss this. It's my favorite ranch job.

~

I stayed with the horses longer than I should have. We're going to have to race to the store to get to my bus in time. But when I get to the house, Margaret's still in bed. Another migraine. There goes my ride. And who's going to take Jane?

I poke my head into Wayne's room. My designated driver is at his desk, hunched over a pile of papers.

"Margaret's in bed with a migraine. We gotta take Jane to the bus," I say. "In forty-five minutes."

"I'm busy," he says. "You take her."

Now I have official permission. It's illegal, but I love it.

As I turn to go, he says, "Don't tell anyone."

~

When I get back from dropping off Jane, I call Samantha. She's been around since Cody was five, but she and Jesse only got married last January. She's a nurse and works at the hospital in Hundred Mile. Her shift doesn't start until two o'clock, so she comes over right away. She's in Margaret's room for about fifteen minutes, then joins me at the kitchen table. I've made tea and a plate of toast. I eat a lot of toast these days.

"I've given Margaret an injection," says Samantha. "It's a kind of sedative that always helps. I think she'll be okay."

"Thanks for coming."

"No problem."

I put a teapot, two mugs, and the toast on the table. "Margaret's migraines are getting worse and worse," I say.

"I know." Samantha stirs sugar into her tea. "I've been thinking about if she should go away for a while."

"What do you mean?"

"Get away from Aspen Lake. Have a little holiday."

"She wouldn't want to do that," I say. "No way."

"I'm not sure about that, Rach. It's hard for Margaret."

"What do you mean 'hard'?" But I know exactly what Samantha means, and it makes me feel guilty because I could do more to help.

Samantha sips her tea and frowns. "Wayne stays home. He doesn't go anywhere. It's Margaret who has to do everything now. She's the ambassador of the family. Don't get me wrong, she loves you all dearly. But I think she needs a break."

I've spread peanut butter on a piece of toast, but now I don't want it. "Margaret would never leave Wayne. Or Jane and me. I know she wouldn't."

"You're probably right. It was just a thought." Samantha drains her tea and carries her mug to the sink. "Do you want a ride into town? You could come with me now and be at school by noon."

"No thanks."

She frowns. "You're missing a lot of classes."

"It's not a big deal. I'm good."

I think she wants to say more, but she doesn't.

"Samantha?"

She pauses at the door to the mudroom.

"Where could Margaret go?"

~

I've started a list.

Margaret's old school friend Joyce who visited from Saskatchewan in her camper last October.

Her older sister Katherine in Ottawa.

I'm stuck there. I call Amber's mom, Susan, and she vetoes both of them. "Katherine severed all ties with the family years ago," she says. "Joyce lives all year round in that camper."

I cross out their names.

"Margaret can have a little getaway with me and Martin," she says. "Our guest room is very quiet."

I don't think Samantha meant High Valley Ranch, which is about a mile down the road. And it's kind of crowded with Amber and Cassie there, too. But I tell Susan it's a nice idea.

Uncle Rob calls from Poland after supper. I commandeer him before Jane takes over with one of her never-ending stories.

"Mom's friends?" says Uncle Rob. "I don't know. I don't think she has a lot. Does she want to go away? I can't imagine Mom leaving the ranch. Are things that bad? Now you're getting me worried. Are you sure she wants to go away?"

"It's hypothetical," I say. "Margaret's fine."

What can Uncle Rob do all the way from Poland?

~

I walk down through the field to the lake where my canoe's upside down on the bank. I flip it over and slide it into the water. Climbing in, I paddle hard, trying to not think about anything, just the paddle. Dipping it in, making a drippy circle of water on the smooth surface.

At our end of the lake, you can't see any other houses. Just forest. On the far side, trees and puffy clouds are reflected in the flat water, perfect upside-down mirror images. In ten minutes, I'm drifting through rustling lily pads near the small grassy point. Last year, loons built a nest here, a small platform made of reeds. They had two adorable babies.

I paddle in closer. A loon is settled on the old nest, its eyes sharp and bright. I stay way back, but it knows I'm here.

A second loon warbles, a long, ripply sound that always gives me goosebumps. It's only a few feet behind my canoe, its sleek black and white head shimmering in the sun. Wayne says the noisy couple might be the same loons that were here last year. You learn about migration in elementary school, but you don't get it until you live in a place like Aspen Lake.

I leave them in peace and paddle around the island. My canoe surges forward with each steady stroke. My arms feel strong. I pass through a school of fish—darting black shadows in the green water. *Focus on the lake*, I tell myself. *Don't think.*

But I do. My mind drifts back to Vancouver. I lived there for almost fifteen years with Mom, six months with Uncle Rob and Aleksandra. I don't think I'd want to live there again. Not after being here. But sometimes the smallness of Aspen Lake sucks. I could walk down the street in Uncle Rob's old neighborhood in the West End of Vancouver and nobody knew if I'd messed up or done something stupid. No one cared anyway. No one even knew my name. In Aspen Lake, everyone knows what everyone else is doing.

In Vancouver, I never stayed in one school long enough to be part of a group. But if we were still living with Uncle Rob, I think I might be by now. I was going to a big high school with hundreds of students. There were lots of different clubs you could join. I'd met some kids at the beach. I even had a boyfriend—sort of. We'd just started going out. Then Jane and I got uprooted again and left.

It's so different here. You just don't have a lot of choice who to be friends with.

I don't really mean that. I have Cody. And I couldn't have a better best friend than Carlee. It just sometimes feels suffocating.

I stop paddling and let my canoe glide. I trail one hand over the side, watching ribbons of silver water stream through my fingers. I miss Mom. Sometimes she screwed up, and she'd get mad over nothing. But lots of times she gave me really good advice. She'd know what to do about this whole mess with Cody. She wouldn't judge me either, even if I am pregnant. I'd give anything for her to be here right now.

~

In the morning, there's an email from Aleksandra. She's a doctor and she went back to Warsaw to work in the hospital there. Uncle Rob kept the apartment, but he's gone to join her. We don't know for how long. It's too late now, but Jane and I think he should have married someone else. Jane despises Aleksandra. Like vanilla ice cream.

Aleksandra's given me links to two wellness retreats. Margaret can go to Greece for two weeks. Unplug and recharge in the fresh air of the Greek mountains for "self-improvement and rediscovery."

Even better, Azores, Portugal. They offer excursions to connect with the land and the environment. Margaret does that every day on our ranch. Doesn't Aleksandra know that?

How would she? She's never even been here. Too busy.

I press reply, type *Maybe*, press send.

Margaret's our ambassador. She stays here.

# CHAPTER TEN

On Friday morning, Carlee sits down at the desk in front of me in French. She spins around and plops a small white paper bag on top of my textbook. "Present."

I peek inside. A pink box. My stomach plummets. My period is now three days overdue. I crumple the bag shut. I jump up and gather my notebook, pens, and textbooks. Madame Laurent will be here any minute.

"Where are you going?" says Carlee. "You never skip French."

"My locker." I need to stash the bag before anyone asks me what's in it.

Emma leans across the aisle. "What's that?"

*Merde!*

"You don't have to thank me," says Carlee to my departing back.

I turn around. "Shush."

She smiles. "But you owe me big time."

~

I've been working at Wagonroad Books since September. Harjit, who's married to my PE teacher, Mr. Minhas, owns the store. Samantha gives me a ride home after her nursing shift at the hospital. Now that Amber and Cassie are back living on High Valley Ranch, I can catch a ride home with Amber, too, when she works late. I love working with Harjit, and I'm saving money for traveling.

Cody's in town tonight, too, playing video games at Derek's, his town friend. He's meeting me here at the bookstore, and we'll walk over to the hospital together. Margaret's added getting a ride home with Cody to the list of things I'm allowed to do while I'm grounded. But that's not for an hour and a half.

Harjit asked me to sort through boxes of donated books for the used section at the back of the store. It's quiet, and as I sort, I tell her about Margaret. After a few minutes, I give up pretending to alphabetize the authors. "I'm not sure I want her to go away. It was horrible when she was in the hospital last year."

"But you managed," says Harjit.

"Barely. Aleksandra thinks Margaret should go to the mountains in Greece or to the Azores in Portugal."

"That woman sounds nuts. Honestly." Harjit blows out air, and we both laugh. I love it when she criticizes Aleksandra.

"Somewhere much closer, I think," says Harjit. "I'll give it some thought."

She helps some customers—a grandmother looking for a birthday present and a man who wants a bird-watching guide. Then she puts the *Sorry We're Closed* sign on the door. I finish the last box of books while she warms up two bowls of *kheer* in the microwave in the storage room. We perch on stools at the front counter.

Kheer is the best. It's like a yummy rice pudding. Harjit puts cardamon in it, and we sprinkle slivered almonds on top.

Harjit brings us something to eat every Friday. Indian food is a rare treat. There are no Indian restaurants in town, and she's usually too busy to cook. Most times, she brings wraps or a platter of sushi from the grocery store.

"This is so delicious," I say.

She smiles. "We better save some for Cody."

Cody and Harjit really like each other. When there are no customers, Harjit watches videos of last year's rodeo with Cody. Cody pretends to like Indian food when he really doesn't.

Kheer is my very favorite, but my throat fills with a hard lump. I've thought of all the people who I'll have to tell if I'm pregnant. I forgot about Harjit.

~

Two postcards from Istanbul in our mailbox.

Jane's postcard is the Blue Mosque. *It really is blue, Jane. On the inside. You can't wear shorts.*

Mine: The Grand Bazaar. *4,000 shops. Craving a Turkish rug but how will I carry it back?*

"Where would you go if you could go anywhere in the world?" I ask.

"The Sahara Desert," says Jane. "Where would you go?"

"Paris."

"Oh my God," she says. "Why do you always say Paris?"

~

Why do I always say Paris?

It's not to see the Eiffel Tower. Though that would be cool—but probably anticlimactic.

When I think of Paris, I think of all the famous writers who lived in drafty cramped apartments and ate bread (*du pain!*) and cheese (*du fromage!*) and hung out in cafés with other starving writers and artists. I'd like to wander around on the cobblestoned streets where they wandered and see what it feels like.

That makes me sound weird, but it's true. Aura says that it's because I read so much and that this is a very romantic vision of Paris that could end up being disappointing. She says if I ever get there, instead of looking for ghosts of dead writers, I should go to a café and write my own book.

I admit that I also binge-watched all the episodes of *Emily in Paris*. I might even find some kids there that are more like me.

My eyes flicker over to my dresser drawer where I stashed the pregnancy test.

*If* I ever get to Paris.

~

I lock the bathroom door, sit on the toilet seat, take the pink box out of the paper bag, and pull out two pink foil pouches and folded paper instructions. My heart is literally pounding like a drum. I read the first part three times. I can't remember a single thing I've read.

Focus. Reread.

*This test is so sensitive that most women have enough of the pregnancy hormone to be detected as early as six days before your period.*

That means I could have got this over with days ago.

*You can use this test any time of the day, though early morning urine is better.*

There are three steps. I tear open one of the pink plastic pouches so I can visualize it.

There's a white wand with a little oval space and a pink cap. I consult the paper. That's called the *result window*. Just in case you're as big a mess as I'm going to be, there's a helpful reminder written on the side. Two lines equals pregnant. One line equals not pregnant. That's pretty clear.

I pull off the cap. There's the stick called the *absorbent tip*.

*Hold the test stick by the thumb grip with the absorbent tip pointing downward and the result window facing away from your body, and place the absorbent tip in your urine stream for five seconds only.*

Got it.

Results in three minutes.

*If you test negative, retest again in a few days.*

What that means is *Don't think you're safe yet*. God.

Jane bangs on the door. "What are you doing in there?"

I stuff everything back in the paper bag. I scan the floor. There's a tiny scrap of pink foil by my feet. I grab it.

I've just learned something about myself: I'm a total coward.

"You're taking ages!" says Jane.

I take one more careful look around.

"Hurry up!" she shouts. "I gotta pee!"

# CHAPTER ELEVEN

The TV flickers. The lights blink off, then on again. Wayne, Margaret, and I are watching the news.

*The BC Wildfire Service reports that more than 200 wildfires are burning in British Columbia after a series of thunderstorms swept over several parts of the province. The majority of these fires are believed to have been caused by lightning.*

Lights blink again.

*This weather pattern is expected to continue for—*

The living room goes dark, the TV screen black.

"Power's out," says Wayne.

We stand by the verandah window. Without the TV, we can hear the wind howling and just make out tree branches lashing back and forth. Jane's been in bed for a few hours. I left a flashlight beside her because they've been predicting this storm all day.

A jagged flash of lightning streaks across the black sky. Thunder crashes. Lucy barks and presses against my legs. Bella stays on the purple couch, whining.

A light bobs across the living room. Jane appears and tucks herself in between Margaret and Wayne. "Can lightning come through a window?" she asks.

Margaret rests her hand on Jane's head. "Of course not."

"This is going to set off more fires," says Wayne.

"But the fires are really far away, right?" says Jane. "Like a thousand miles."

Another flash of lightning, followed almost instantly by thunder. You can count the seconds to figure out where it is, but we don't need to. It's right on top of our house. Bella howls.

Our ranch is surrounded by forest.

"If we stay by this window, watching, if we don't look away, we can protect our trees," I tell Jane. "We just can't let our guard down."

"Sort of like a game?" says Jane.

I wish it was.

After what seems like forever, the lightning stops. The wind dies down, and it's so quiet.

"That's over for tonight," says Wayne.

"I'm not going back to bed all by myself," says Jane.

Wayne lights the oil lamps. Margaret brings out cocoa and banana bread.

~

3 A.M.

Google search:

*Lightning is a giant spark of electricity in the atmosphere. It is hotter than the sun. When lightning hits a tree, the heat vaporizes any water in its path, causing the tree to explode.*

I put my iPad down and stare out my bedroom window, shivering in my nightie. It's been hours since the lightning storm, but I search the blackness for a flame bursting into life in the night forest. I search for exploding trees.

~

Cody's on his way. I didn't ask him to come, but I didn't say no, either, when he said he could get a ride with Jesse. What reason could I give? Sunday afternoon is still officially the weekend, but Margaret says I'm not grounded anymore. I couldn't come up with anything else that sounded believable.

I can't act normal with Cody right now. All I can think about is my stupid period. And there's still the ring. I have no clue what to do about that. I'm lying on my bed, staring at it. Every time I take it out of its box, it looks bigger and more expensive. Then I hear Jesse's truck. I put the ring back in its box and bury it under T-shirts in my bottom dresser drawer. I head downstairs.

At first, it's awkward. But probably just to me. Cody's the same as ever. He looks great, his shaggy hair messed up, and he's so tanned. My heart gives a little jump. We take lemonade and a deck of cards out to the verandah.

While Cody's dealing, I say, "How was Emma's party?"

"Would've been better with you. Everyone wondered where you were."

I'll decide later if I believe that.

"How's Acorn doing?" I ask.

"Great. Getting stronger every day. Cheyenne's a perfect mom."

We're just sitting here, talking about stuff. This is nice. I smile at Cody.

He smiles back. Then Jane staggers out, carrying a big cardboard box.

"Look what I found in the shed," she says.

Dusty wooden mallets with colored stripes are sticking out the top. She drops the box, and it splits apart, colored wooden balls skittering across the verandah floor.

"That's a croquet set," says Cody.

"Croquet!" Jane's intrigued. "Like Alice and the Queen play in *Alice in Wonderland*!"

"If you say so." Cody gets up. "Let's play."

"Me too!" says Jane. "I'm playing, too!"

"Choose your weapons." Cody pulls out a green mallet and swings it in the air. "Your ball and the mallet have to be the same color."

Sweat is already trickling down my back. "Isn't it kind of hot to play croquet?"

Cody paces around the lawn while Jane follows, sticking wire hoops into the grass. It seems random at first, but it turns into a crooked pattern. At the very end, Cody hammers a wooden post into the ground with a mallet.

"You know how to play this?" I ask.

"Yes. Okay, basically, whoever gets their ball through all the hoops first and hits the post wins. But there are some rules."

Cody can't remember most of them.

We settle on: Wait for your turn. Don't use your hands. Don't hit anyone with your mallet.

A short delay—Jane still can't make up her mind between purple and blue. She finally takes purple. I'm green, Cody's red.

Jane goes first. Three wild swings! The last one just misses Cody's head. He ducks. "Keep your mallet down! You're not playing golf."

Two more swings, then smack! Her purple ball flies over the top of three hoops into Margaret's flower bed. "Whoa!" she says. "Good shot!"

We send her back to the beginning. We add a new rule: You can't skip hoops.

Cody and Jane bash their way around, arguing and blasting each other's balls in all directions. I play a strategic game, gentle nudges, sizing up each hoop carefully.

Cody's winning, and I'm bringing up the rear when Jane's ball whacks Cody in the middle of his back.

"That's it!" he shouts. "This is war!"

Something acrid is tickling my nose. Smoke? Margaret hasn't lit the woodstove for days. And the sky is blue. But now I'm sure I'm smelling smoke.

"Cody, do you smell—"

They're not listening. Jane brandishes her purple mallet like a sword, shrieking, "Off with your head!"

The smell, whatever it was, disappears. I collapse on the grass and watch the battle.

Jane and I adore the Queen in *Alice in Wonderland.* She uses live hedgehogs for balls and live flamingos for mallets. She decapitates players for missing their turns.

But she's no match for Jane.

# CHAPTER TWELVE

The dogs have been barking for ten minutes. I'm lying on my bed, not looking at the drawer with the pregnancy test. It's called avoidance. I'm brilliant at avoidance, but right now it's not working. I feel sick.

When I can't stand it any longer, I get up and go see what's going on. Margaret's just coming out of her garden. "There's something wrong with the water," she says. "There's barely a trickle.... What is *wrong* with those dogs? Would someone please make them stop barking?"

I turn around helplessly and shout, "Jane!"

"I'm playing!" she hollers back, from somewhere on the far side of the garden fence. "In my swamp."

"Get over here!"

Jane prances around the corner of the fence, bare feet and legs splattered with mud, shorts soaking wet. Bella pads behind her, her golden legs muddy, and Lucy, equally muddy, bounds in circles. "Go and find Papa," I say. "Tell him we need him in the garden. Pronto. And don't let the dogs in the house!"

Wayne trudges out, turns the tap on and off a few times, then disappears into the pump house by the barn. Margaret and I lug buckets of water from the kitchen to the garden while Jane stands guard at the hose.

"The water's stopped totally now!" she says.

Wayne's back, a wrench in his hand. "I tightened up some joints. I've fixed it."

"No," says Margaret, "you haven't fixed it. There's still no water in my garden. Did you hear me? No water."

"What?" says Wayne.

"It's the old pipes. Everything on this ranch is old." I've never heard Margaret sound so helpless. "Look at all the rotted fences. And the barn's practically tipping over."

"The barn's tipping over?" says Jane.

"Now you just wait a minute," starts Wayne.

"It's true," says Margaret. "Everything's falling apart."

"Is the barn tipping over?" says Jane.

"It is not tipping over!" roars Wayne. "It's sagging. That's what old buildings do. But it'll be here for another hundred years because your great-grandfather Joseph built it."

"Well, I won't be here for another hundred years, but I would appreciate a few more years of water for my plants," says Margaret. "If that's not too much to ask. And now I'm going in the house because I'm not going to stay out here any longer and watch my garden die while you defend your Bird forefathers."

Jane's head swivels back and forth between Margaret and Wayne. I stay out of it. This is their fight, not mine.

"You mean the house that my father built!" Wayne shouts after her. "You don't seem to mind that."

~

Wayne's back in the pump house. I check on him in between watering vegetables and trips to the house to fill more buckets. He's turning faucets and poking at black pipes that crisscross the ceiling.

"What are you doing in here?" I ask.

"What does it look like I'm doing?" He stares at the sea of pipes. "There's gotta be a leak in the waterline that goes to the garden. How the blazes am I going to find that? The damn line's buried underground. It probably goes all over the place. It wasn't planned well. And you don't need to tell Margaret that."

If I were my great-grandfather Joseph Bird, and I was burying a waterline, where would I bury it?

Wait a sec.

In the middle of a heat wave, when all the cows' watering holes have dried up, when everything is parched, when even the lake level is low, Jane has a swamp?

~

In a dip in the lawn, between the pump house and the far corner of the garden fence, Old Faithful is bubbling up through the ground.

Wayne produces a shovel. I sigh and start to dig. He shuts off all the water in the pump house because my hole keeps filling with water.

I keep digging.

Under the grass, there's a microscopic layer of dirt and then it's solid rock. Our Bird forefathers built this ranch in the middle of a gravel quarry.

"We need Cody," says Wayne. "Too bad Cody's not here."

What century is Wayne living in? And he might not be so excited to have Cody's help if he knew about the pregnancy kit in the upstairs bathroom (in the house his father built).

Jane crouches beside the hole. "How far are you gonna dig?"

I stand up and try to straighten my back.

"It's just a damn shame I can't do this myself," says Wayne. "When I think how many holes I've dug putting in fence posts, this would be nothing. If Cody—"

I go back to work. My shovel strikes something that doesn't clang like a rock. I squat. It's a piece of black plastic pipe with a thick root wrapped partly around it, a jagged crack across the middle.

"Found it!" I shout.

Basically, the root made its way secretly underground all the way from a huge fir tree at the edge of the lawn and strangled the water pipe. With Wayne firing out orders and my newly acquired exhaust pipe skills, I manage to repair it with wire, a clamp, and an L-shaped piece of plastic pipe from the workshop.

I connect the sprinkler. Jane and I watch the water arching over the garden. For the first time in days, I'm proud of something I've done. It feels good. I should fix more things.

The feeling lasts about two seconds.

How am I going to fix things if I have a baby?

"I want that hole filled in," says Wayne. "I'm not going to look at a hole in the middle of my grass all summer."

"It's making a rainbow!" says Jane.

"Get Nana," I say.

~

I opened my bedroom window wide before I went to bed. Now arctic air is blasting in my face. I yank up the blanket crumpled by my feet and hug my knees.

I'm still freezing. And I'm wide awake. I get up and cross the room to close my window.

Two lights bob outside in the dark. Someone's in the garden. In the middle of the night?

I put on my fleece robe and slippers and head downstairs. There's one flashlight left in the mudroom. I grab it and head outside. The grass crunches under my feet.

I hear them before I get there.

"The beans," says Margaret's voice. "We've got to cover the beans."

"I can't find the damn beans." Wayne, somewhere in the dark. Then the sound of something crashing over (A watering pail? Bigger than that. A wheelbarrow?), a muttered curse, and "This garden is a bloody obstacle course. Margaret, why don't you ever put things away?"

I go through the open gate, beam my flashlight around, and find Margaret. She's wearing pajamas and her green garden clogs but no robe. Her arms are full of white cloths. She points her flashlight right into my eyes.

"It's Rachel, Wayne!"

Wayne appears, his light wobbly, and we huddle together. Wayne's in pajamas, too, no robe, and bare feet.

"Where are your shoes?" I ask.

"No time," he says. "Margaret was in such a damn hurry. I had to run after her."

"Are you completely crazy? Do you want your toes amputated from frostbite? Go inside. *Now.*"

He stomps off, muttering. I take over. The lettuce and spinach and peas will survive. The beans are the problem, they hate frost. And Margaret is passionate about her beans.

We maneuver up and down the paths. Margaret points with her flashlight, and I drape the white cloths over the little plants.

When we get back inside, I make cocoa. We huddle at the table, wrapped in blankets, Wayne's feet soaking in a tub of warm water.

"You're both going to get pneumonia," I say. "That's a given."

"It was still so warm when I went to bed," says Margaret. "I thought...it's one degree below freezing now. I can't believe I missed that coming." Tears well up in her eyes and leak down her cheeks. "I'm always so careful. I don't know what happened."

This is by far the worst part of the whole night. Margaret just doesn't cry. Ever.

"Now you stop that right now, Margaret." Wayne's hand, holding his mug of cocoa, is shaking. "We saved your beans."

At that moment, they stop being my grandparents and they turn into two old people, shivering in the kitchen. And I have this sudden, terrifying thought. Jane's seven. When she's my age, Wayne and Margaret will be in their eighties. What will happen to her? She has to grow up here. And me? After I've traveled the planet? I have to have somewhere to come home to.

That's assuming I'll be able to travel. But even if I don't have a baby, I could never leave Jane anywhere but here. What if there is no *here* anymore? My mind goes into overdrive. Our ranch could burn up in a forest fire. Margaret and Wayne could get really sick. They could end up in a nursing home, or they could die. Why didn't I ever think of this before? Our whole life here is so fragile. It could fall apart overnight.

Jane comes in, sleepy.

"I want cocoa, too," she says.

What would Jane and I do without Wayne and Margaret?

~

I break my rule and let Jane come back to bed with me. "Get in," I say, "and don't hog all the room."

She's under the covers in a flash.

I take off my robe and slippers. "No talking. We're going to sleep."

"Can I just say one thing?"

"No."

"Just one thing."

"Double no."

"Please, please, please."

"What?"

"There's blood on your nightie."

# CHAPTER THIRTEEN

I find Carlee by her locker, grab her hand, and haul her into the girls' bathroom. Thank God, it's empty.

"Where were you?" I say. "I was texting you all night!"

"Dad confiscated my phone," she says. "Long story. But just for twenty-four hours. What's happened?"

I can barely get the words out. "I'm okay…I mean, I'm not…. Wait." I peer under the row of cubicle doors to make sure we're really alone. "I'm not pregnant!"

Carlee grabs me in an enormous hug. We hold each other and rock back and forth.

"When did you find out?" she says. "Did you take the test?"

"Nope. My…it started last night. And guess what?" I give a shaky laugh. "I've got the worst cramps ever."

"Cramps are good!" says Carlee. "Cramps are fantastic!"

"Easy for you to say." Carlee never gets cramps.

"Would you rather have morning sickness?" she says.

I start to cry.

~

The leaves on all the tiny bean plants are black. Margaret knows, but she doesn't come back to the garden until it's almost time for Jane to go to bed.

"What are you two doing?" she says.

Jane and I are crouched side by side on the path.

"Planting new beans," says Jane.

We found packets of bean seeds in the garden shed. We dug furrows in the soft black soil. I pass Jane a bean, she pops it into the ground.

We're a bean-planting factory.

~

I'm reading *Little House in the Big Woods* to Jane. I promised her that when it's not so hot, we'll go down to the old house and play pioneers. We get to the end of the chapter. "Now scram. I'm going to read my own book for a while. Then I'll help you get ready for bed."

"Can I sleep in Amber's T-shirt?" she says. "Please, please, please."

Amber gave me the T-shirt for my birthday. It's turquoise with *I'm sorry, did I roll my eyes out loud?* written across the front. Love that sarcasm.

"Just for tonight," I say. "It's in my bottom drawer."

Jane leaps off my bed.

Then I leap off my bed, too. "Wait! I'll get it...."

Too late. Jane's rummaging in my pile of T-shirts. She holds up the small ring box. "What's this?"

Shit.

"Nothing to—"

She pulls off the lid. "Wow!" She takes out the ring and slides it onto her thumb. It fits perfectly. "Where did you get it?"

"Cody."

"Are you getting married?"

"No," I say.

Her eyes are wide. "It's like a princess' ring. You could be in a fairy tale."

"Except I don't believe in fairy tales."

Jane turns her thumb this way and that, admiring my glittering ring. "Me and Cassie do."

"Good for you," I say. "Get ready to be disappointed."

"Why?"

"You'll find out when you're older. Now put it back."

"Would you like the ring more if it was a diamond?"

"Of course not," I say. "It's my birthstone. An emerald. That's even better. But it's not a real emerald before you get all excited. That would cost a fortune."

"It's fake, then," says Jane. "But I wouldn't care. It's still so beautiful. Can I take it to show-and-tell?"

"No."

"Can I show Nana and Papa?"

"No."

"Can I just tell Nana and Papa?"

"No."

"Can I please, please, please wear it just for tonight?"

"No."

Jane blows out air. "Then why do you even have it?"

# CHAPTER FOURTEEN

Cody's been on his phone for ages, leaning against a post by the front door of the school. Carlee and Emma are sitting cross-legged on the pavement, playing some kind of hand game from elementary school. Tyson just grabbed Dai's baseball cap, and Dai's chasing him across the strip of grass.

Why is everyone so annoying today? Or maybe they're not annoying. Maybe it's me. We're waiting for Sarah, then we're heading to A&W.

"Jesus," says Cody suddenly. "They've canceled the Aspen Lake Rodeo."

"What?" Tyson tosses Dai his cap. "Dude, for real?"

"Show me that." Carlee jumps up and grabs Cody's phone. Her long black hair swings over her face. "Shit."

The Aspen Lake rodeo is always at the end of July at the rodeo grounds. It's a huge deal. Cowboys come from as far away as Alberta and Washington.

"Why did they cancel it?" says Emma.

"Because there's going to be a stupid heat dome," says Cody.

"What the hell is a heat dome?" says Tyson. "They cancel a rodeo because it's hot? That's insane."

"Can they do that?" Carlee sounds so indignant. "Without taking a vote or something?"

Cody still looks shocked. "Well, they just did."

"It's bullshit," says Dai.

Carlee wraps her arms around Cody in a tight hug. They stay like that for a long time. Should I be worried about that? My gut tells me no. I totally trust them. The rodeo has everything to do with them and nothing to do with me. This year, Cody was all psyched to compete in the adult section for steer riding. And Carlee gets barrel racing points toward a championship every time she rides.

Everyone's talking at the same time. And I have a very disloyal thought. All you see on the news these days are the fires. It's intense. People's houses are burning up. They're losing everything. Isn't that just a tiny bit more important than a rodeo?

"It's not like they canceled it forever," I say. "It'll be back next year." Stupid! Everyone stares at me, so I blunder on. "Maybe it's too dangerous to have a rodeo right now. What about the horses and the cows? I mean, can't they get heat stroke or something?" I feel sick if I think of Magic running during a heat dome.

"We know how to look after our animals, Rachel," says Carlee. "Once they're out of the ring, they're in shade, and we have misting stations everywhere."

Cody's looking at me as if I'm a stranger. Like I'm not one of them.

This happens all the time. I'm the newbie who doesn't get it. They've probably been going to the rodeo together since they were in Grade One.

Emma's phone dings. "Sarah's not coming. Let's go."

"I'm going to pass," I say. It's hot, and they're going to walk along the side of the highway. Baking pavement and no shade. No one else seems to mind. "I've got a headache."

"You sure?" says Cody, but he's miles away in rodeo land.

"Yeah. See you later."

I kiss him, then they're gone.

But I do hear Tyson's parting comment to Dai. "Like she really cares."

That's mean and unfair. I do care. I watch Cody and Carlee lagging behind the others talking. Then I wander back inside the school.

I'm not sure what I want to do. I go to the library and find it's deserted except for two girls doing homework. I retreat into a quiet corner and flop down on some big floor pillows.

But for once, I can't get into my book. I shut it and close my eyes, worrying about what I've just done.

At lunch, we always meet at the front door of the school before walking into town. On the days when Cody and Carlee aren't here, I always have to get there quickly. I never think the others will wait for me. They'll wait for Sarah or Dai or whoever, but they won't wait for me. And then today, I say I don't want to go. That wasn't a good move.

I do have a headache, that was true, and I didn't feel like sitting in A&W. But I should've gone.

~

"Margaret Bird never cries," says Harjit.

"I know."

"I've been doing some thinking." She flips open her laptop, taps the keyboard, and the screen fills with ocean surrounded by forest. The words *Hummingbird Haven* are at the top.

"It's on Saltspring Island," she says. "My cousin went there, and she raved about it. It's a special place. Just for women."

She scrolls down through images of little cabins in the trees, a group of women doing yoga by the water, a shady forest trail. "'Relax your mind, body, and soul,'" she reads. "You think Margaret would like that?"

Of course she would like that. Who wouldn't? But the truth is, I don't really want her to leave us.

So I say, "I don't know. It looks okay, but we've got forest and nature and all that stuff on the ranch. No ocean, but we've got the lake. How would this be different?"

"It would absolutely be different. No one knows Margaret on Saltspring Island. She could be anonymous."

"'Good morning rituals of journaling, meditation, yoga,'" I read. "That sounds very un-Margaret to me."

"You might be surprised."

There's more.

*Take care of your personal growth.* I swallow. I don't want Margaret to change. I just want her the way she used to be.

*Come here to feel safe.*

That just makes me feel scared.

Then there's a picture of a beautiful garden. Sunflowers, daisies, roses. A lump fills up my throat.

"Margaret should go," I say.

"I think so, too."

Harjit's closing the store for a week, and then I'll be out of school. This is my last work night until September. She glances at her watch. "It'd be wonderful if you could get the new shipment shelved tonight."

"I can do that."

"I'm going to miss you tons," she says. "Promise to pop in and say hi when you're in town?"

"Promise. Harjit, before I do the books, could we phone Hummingbird Haven?"

~

Amber's working late in town, and I catch a ride home with her. She's got her new car—a bright orange Toyota Rav4 with all the high-tech gadgets. She bought it a month ago. It still smells like new leather.

I settle into the passenger seat. After walking along the burning sidewalk, it's heaven. I love air conditioning.

"Jesus, it's hot today," says Amber. "They keep saying a heat dome's coming. Is that going to be even hotter than this? God."

She's heard about the rodeo, so I fill her in on Hummingbird Haven.

"That's a great idea!" she says. "Mom's been worrying about Margaret."

"Amber." I pause, trying to formulate my words. "Do you ever think about what will happen to High Valley Ranch when your parents can't run it anymore?"

"Where'd that come from?"

"I'm just wondering. Do you?"

"Sometimes," she says slowly. "Why?"

"I don't know. I've been thinking about Margaret and Wayne. What if something happens to them? They could die. Wayne's already had one heart attack. Where would Jane go?"

Amber glances sideways at me. "Rachel, honestly. Do you sit up at night deliberately thinking of crazy things to worry about?"

"Seriously, where would Jane go?"

"Seriously? She'd live with me and Cassie. You, too."

I'm quiet, watching the trees through the side window until they all blur together. I'm thinking about what Amber said, trying to imagine it, and feeling choked up. Amber's amazing. Finally, I say, "Did you just think that up right now?"

"Yeah."

We both laugh.

We make a quick stop at the Aspen Lake store. No SASE today, no postcards. When we get to the gravel road, Amber pulls over and stops. "It's time you drove something besides that old pickup."

"What? You'll let me drive your new car?"

The Rav is her second child.

We get out, switch sides. "It's zippy," she says. "You don't need a lot of gas. Just don't hit any trees. I haven't got any dings on this thing yet."

I creep along, steering around a huge cow patty.

"More gas than that."

I speed up.

There's a cloud of dust in the rearview mirror.

# CHAPTER FIFTEEN

"I'll bring up the site to show you." I'm perched on Wayne's unmade bed, laptop ready. He's at his desk in his pajamas, immersed in old cattle magazines. My timing's important. He's heading for bed soon and won't get a chance to talk to Margaret until tomorrow.

"Saltspring Island is a hippie-dippie place," he says. "Not a chance Margaret would want to go there."

"I think she will."

I clear a spot and set the laptop in front of him.

"A little island overrun with vegetarians eating tofu?" Wayne is forever loyal to the cattle ranchers of this world. "What the hell would she do there?"

"Um…yoga, meditation, Reiki…." I switch tactics. "She can experiment with different ways to garden, learn about unusual plants."

"They won't grow here anyway." Wayne shuffles papers.

"Margaret going away was Samantha's idea." I let that sink in because Wayne admires Samantha. "Margaret's our ambassador. She goes into town, does all the shopping, the banking, goes to the post office."

"Like she's always done," says Wayne. "That's what your grandmother does. What's your point?"

I don't say anything. It always unnerves Wayne when I don't say anything. Finally, he mutters, "Is Margaret sick? Is that what you're thrashing about trying to tell me?"

"No, she's not sick. But she's really tired. She's getting chronic headaches. She needs a chance to rest."

"Rest? It's spring, for Christ's sake. Margaret doesn't want to rest. She's got her garden." Wayne pushes his hands through his ruffled gray hair. "Does Margaret even know about this?"

"Kind of."

"I didn't think so," he says. "I'll talk to her."

Not before me.

~

"This place doesn't sound at all like me," says Margaret. "Meditation? Yoga. I don't think so."

"You'd love it," I say. "An island. How cool is that?"

She smiles. "I know someone who moved to Saltspring. Barbie Wilson. We were very close once, went to high school together in Clinton. We sent Christmas cards back and forth for years, but then we stopped. She used to send me photos of her tea roses. I love my roses, but you can only grow the really hardy kinds in Aspen Lake. Our winters would kill tea roses."

Margaret's torn. I can tell. I'm on the right track. "Why didn't you say so before?" I say. "You could visit her."

"If she's still there. I'm going back a long way."

"This is meant to be."

Margaret squeezes my hand. "You're a dear girl to think of this, but it wouldn't work. You'd have to look after my garden, and you're busy with school. The garden takes up a lot of time."

"I can do it."

"And then there's Jane."

"What about her?" We both know that I've looked after Jane my whole life.

"And, of course, Wayne would have to agree," she says.

"He will. Harjit called, and they've had a last-minute cancelation. There's one spot available and you can go next Thursday."

"Thursday? Oh, I don't think so. How would I get there?"

"We'll figure that out. There's one more thing, you sort of have to make a commitment. They don't want drop-ins. They want people to commit. But that's no big deal."

"What kind of commitment?" says Margaret. "One week? That's as long as I'd want to be away. If I even agree to this."

"Two."

~

When I get up in the morning, Wayne and Margaret are sitting together on the purple couch in the living room talking. I have the feeling they've been talking for a long time.

"Susan called," says Margaret. "Amber told her about Saltspring. She's been wanting to go to Vancouver to see her sister. She'll take me down to the ferry and come back for me later. She says she doesn't mind at all."

"So, you're going?"

"It looks like it." Margaret's beaming. "I can't quite believe it. I'm feeling very guilty about this, but your grandfather has talked me into it."

"Of course you're going," he says. "I'm not taking no for an answer. It's high time you had a holiday."

They smile at each other.

Then Margaret frowns. "I'll have to think of the best way to tell Jane," she says.

# CHAPTER SIXTEEN

Samantha arrives when we're still at the kitchen table finishing breakfast. Wayne's starting a new arthritis medication. She's brought the pills, a blood pressure cuff, and a little chart.

She has a cup of coffee and shows Jane how the blood pressure cuff works while I wash dishes. Wayne finishes his toast, then stands up. "There's nothing wrong with my blood pressure," he says. "I have excellent blood pressure."

"Then you won't fuss when I take it now," says Samantha.

Wayne slumps back in his chair and pulls up the sleeve of his plaid shirt. Samantha wraps the black cuff around his upper arm. "Rest your elbow on the table and don't fidget."

She presses a button; the cuff whirrs and inflates, then collapses with a sigh. "127 over 70," she says to Margaret. "I'm happy with that."

"What did I tell you?" says Wayne.

Samantha fills in the time and date and the blood pressure numbers on the chart. She's also brought a large index card where she's printed:

*Good: 125/70*
*Not so good: 145/85*
*Worrying: 150/90*
*Very worrying: 160/100*

"I'll leave everything here with the new pills," she says. "You need to take your blood pressure every morning for two weeks, Wayne. Are you keeping yourself cool?"

"We've got fans in most of the rooms," says Margaret.

"Take my blood pressure," says Jane. "Please, please, please. And use my good arm."

She's never said that before. *My good arm.*

When Jane was three, she spilled boiling water on her shoulder and arm when she was making Mr. Noodles. I was there, just in the other room, and I should have prevented it. I didn't. She'll have the burn scars forever.

She yanks her T-shirt up over her knobby shoulder, watches the black cuff while it whirrs and goes up and down.

"Ninety-six over sixty," says Samantha.

"Is that good?" asks Jane.

"Very good."

"Why does Papa get to have higher numbers than me?"

"Because Papa is old."

Samantha sticks the chart and the paper with the numbers on the fridge with magnets. "We could smell smoke at our place this morning," she says.

"I thought I smelled smoke when I was in the garden," says Margaret. "It's been breezy all day. There's a big fire near Quesnel. It might have been coming from there."

"It's an east wind," says Wayne. "Any smoke's coming from the Slack Lake fire."

"Well, thank the Lord it's not near us," says Margaret.

~

Jesse's barbecuing ribs tonight and I'm invited. "No rush, Rachel," says Samantha. "I'm going to go out and have a look at the garden with Margaret."

I go upstairs, change from my shorts into jeans, and put on a sky blue tank top. Hair in a loose braid down my back. Riding boots.

I glance at my dresser, hesitate. The ring. It's just not fair to keep it.

My heart's beating faster, trying to imagine how this is going to go. Should I give it back before dinner or after dinner? Definitely not in front of Jesse and Samantha. We need to be alone. If I give it back, does that mean we're breaking up? Can you even give a ring back and not break up? What are the rules? Even thinking about breaking up makes me feel sick. That's not what I want. Not now. I just don't want the ring.

But what if I give it back to Cody and he says, "Okay, that's it, we're breaking up." Do I dare risk that?

Aura swears by writing things down. I sit down at my desk, put the ring box in front of me, and get out a piece of paper and a pen.

**IF I GIVE BACK THE RING AND CODY WANTS TO BREAK UP**

1. **Will I be lonely?**
2. **Will Cody hate me?**
3. **Will Carlee be mad at me?**
4. **Will I still be in the group?**

**IF I KEEP THE RING AND WE DON'T BREAK UP**

1. **I'll still be in the group.**
2. **Carlee will still be my best friend.**
3. **Will I have to wear it?**

I don't feel better. I feel worse. My stomach's in knots. I take the ring out and slip it onto my finger. It really is beautiful. I wish I wanted it.

I put it in its box, put the box in the drawer, and head downstairs. I'm afraid to give it back because I'm afraid of what Cody will do.

# CHAPTER SEVENTEEN

"Cody's out in the round pen with Banjo," says Jesse.

Banjo's a big bay horse, three years old, with some very bad habits. He belongs to one of Cody's cousins. No one's ridden him yet.

A round pen is a small corral for training horses. I can hear pounding hoofbeats as I approach. Dust churns up. Cody's in with Banjo, holding a thick coiled rope against his thigh. Banjo's galloping in a tight circle, nostrils flaring. His dark neck is slick with sweat. He slows and then bucks hard, and Cody swings the rope at his hind end. Banjo picks up a steady, fast canter.

Carlee's watching from outside the pen, leaning against the top rail. She turns. "Hey, Rach."

"I didn't know you were here," I say. "Hi, Cody!"

He nods, totally focused on Banjo.

I stand beside Carlee. "How come you didn't tell me you were coming?"

"Last-minute thing," she says. "Dad's measuring a new dock for someone in Aspen Lake."

Carlee's dad is a carpenter. Carlee's like the rest of us, always bumming rides to places.

"I'm trying to learn this round pen stuff," she says. "Cody says it would be good training for my horse, too."

Banjo skids to a halt and spins, swinging his hind end toward Cody, kicking out hard. More rope from Cody, and the horse swivels around and gallops in another circle. "See that, Carlee?" he says. "When I ask him to turn, he has to turn his head into me, not away."

Cody's explained how this works to me. It's all about more pressure and less pressure and controlling movement.

"Less pressure is always better." He's talking to Carlee, not me. "If you want your horse to be responsive."

Less pressure is better. That could be a good rule for life. I'm trying to decide if I mind Carlee being here. I don't.

Cody drops the rope and Banjo lowers his head, lips chewing. Cody makes a kissing sound, and Banjo walks right up to him. Cody strokes his foam-flecked neck.

"That's so cool, Cody," says Carlee. "He's really respecting you."

"He's doing good."

There's a saddle and saddle blanket leaning against the fence. "You're not going to ride him today, are you?" I say.

"Nope, I just want him to get used to the way the saddle feels." Cody's always so patient around horses. "First, I'm going to send him around the pen a few more times. You wanna come in and try, Carlee?"

Carlee will be good at this. That I know for sure. When Cody and Carlee get talking horses, I always find myself drifting away. I love riding and I love Magic, absolutely, but I'm not into the training part as much as them.

"I'm going to go see if I can help Samantha," I say.

I take a quick detour to see Cheyenne and Acorn. The colt is stockier now, still just as cute. I give him his favorite treat, a back scratch.

Jesse's got the barbecue going. A row of baked potatoes wrapped in tinfoil sit on the warming rack. It's a perfect night to eat outside. The table is an old barn door with peeling red paint, balanced on four log rounds. Samantha has hung mosquito traps from the nearby trees. It's too early in the summer for wasps. Strings of Japanese lanterns glow overhead.

I finish making the coleslaw. The trailer has a tiny kitchen so Samantha's very organized. I'm setting out plates and cutlery on the table when Carlee and Cody get back, laughing about something.

"Good timing!" says Jesse. He's carrying two lawn chairs. "Cody, can you get a couple more of these from the porch?"

"What can I do?" says Carlee.

"You can run over to the Big House and tell Lois and Kit we're eating in five minutes."

~

Cody's grandparents walk across the grass holding hands, which is very sweet. Kit is a big man, like Wayne, with a tanned face all year round. I've never seen him without his cowboy hat. Lois is small and wiry with a cloud of bluish-white hair. She calls everyone "dear" except Kit. She's the only one who calls Kit by his real name, Christopher.

Everyone grabs a seat. I carry out the coleslaw and a brown paper bag of warm rolls. Samantha brings out a butter dish, a bowl of sour cream and bacon bits, and a roll of paper towels.

I sit beside Lois, opposite Carlee and Cody. Everyone digs in, and it's quiet. I really hate the messy part of ribs, but they taste yummy.

At the head of the table, Kit tilts his cowboy hat back and gives his mouth a final wipe. "Nothing like a plate of fine beef ribs. The Good Lord was thinking straight when he made the first steer."

Carlee rolls her eyes at me.

"Cody," says Kit, "I'm looking forward to the day when you're riding the range with your dad and me. Three generations of Cooper men."

"We hardly ride the range anymore, Dad," says Jesse. "We use ATVs."

"Cody's smart," says Samantha. "He should be the first Cooper to go to university."

Cody's wiping his plate with a bun. "I've figured out what I want to do," he says. "And it doesn't include going to university. Sorry, Sam."

"Thank the Lord for that," says Kit. "These days, a diploma's not worth the paper it's written on. You need a real—"

"And it doesn't include running a herd of cattle. I know that's what you want, but it's not for me, Grandpa. I'm going to raise quarter horses. And you're wrong, Dad. An ATV can't replace a good cutting horse."

How does Cody do that? Sound so calm, so sure of what he wants? I'd be a mess trying to stand up to someone like Kit.

Kit frowns. "Listen, son. Only the big spreads make a go of breeding. They've got their fancy breeding operations, their studs and mares and a vet all year round. Even then, most of them have to do other things to break even, give lessons, trail rides, board horses, shit like that."

"Language, Christopher! In front of the kids!" says Lois. Cody always says his grandmother thinks he's still ten.

"I just don't want to see Cody make a mistake," says Kit.

"There's more than one way to do things," says Cody. "I've got ideas. Rachel and I have talked about it."

Carlee shoots me a questioning look. Did we talk about it? Not really. He brought it up. I don't think I was even very supportive. Now he's making it sound like we're going to do this together. Yikes.

"Whatever you decide to do, dear, you'll do well," says Lois.

"Thanks, Grandma," says Cody.

"It's a rich man's game." Kit's pissed off. "You'll end up in the poorhouse."

~

Carlee's dad picks her up after dinner. The sun's low in the sky, and it's cooled off enough for Cody and me to go for a ride. Cody saddles Flight, his roan gelding, and I saddle Jesse's mare, Lady. She's a palomino, six, dainty, and skittish. We ride along the fence line, up through the fields.

We pass through a gate and onto a wide, grassy road that leads up to where Jesse and Kit cut wood. We ride side by side. "So, you're serious about raising quarter horses?" I say.

"Yeah," he says. "Do you have a problem with that?"

"I sort of do. It's like there's pressure on me to want to do it, too."

"That's ridiculous. You can do what you want, Rachel. We don't have to do everything the same."

That makes me feel better, and I think he means it. Anyway, it's so far away, and it's stupid to be worrying about it right now.

A doe pops out of the bushes, ears high, tail twitching. Lady swoops sideways, and my heart jumps.

"You okay?" asks Cody.

"Yup."

"Ready?"

The ground's even here, good footing, no gopher holes.

"Ready."

I press my heels gently against Lady's side, and she responds instantly. She feels light in my hands, galloping hard but under control. A year ago, I wouldn't have dared ride a horse like this.

We slow our horses to a canter and then a trot. We turn up a trail, Cody and Flight leading. Just ahead, there's a mossy, fallen tree across the path. I prepare, leaning forward on Lady's neck, pressing my thighs against the saddle.

Flight soars over the log, Cody and his horse like one. It's my turn. Lady shortens her stride. Too much. I squeeze with my heels, and we pop over easily.

Cody's grinning at me, and I grin right back.

We come out into a grassy meadow and gallop again, hooves thundering. I don't want to fight with Cody anymore. I don't want to worry about anything. It can be so good when we're together. Like it is right now.

# CHAPTER EIGHTEEN

"What's the suitcase for?" says Jane.

I'm washing our breakfast dishes at the kitchen sink while Margaret works on a long grocery list at the table. We've been brainstorming meals that she could make in the next few days and freeze. My top picks are spaghetti sauce and chili.

"Why were you in my room, Jane?" says Margaret calmly.

"Looking for you." Jane frowns. "Why do you have a suitcase? Are you going somewhere?"

"Come and sit here and I'll explain," says Margaret.

Jane doesn't budge from the doorway. "Where are you going?"

"A little island called Saltspring."

"Why?"

"Just for a holiday."

"When?"

Margaret hesitates. "Thursday."

"Like this Thursday?" says Jane.

"Yes."

"In five days." Jane's fast.

"I'm going to be right beside a beach and I'm going to hunt for some really pretty shells for you," says Margaret.

"I don't like shells," says Jane.

I step in. "Yes, you—"

Margaret frowns. "Rachel, stop. Jane, I want you to sit down and tell me what kinds of cookies to put on the grocery list."

"Cookies are stupid." Jane's face is smoldering. "And you're stupid, Nana!"

She's still in the doorway, where she can make a run for it. Just in case.

"That was mean, Jane," I say. "You should be so glad that Nana's having a holiday. You should say you're sorry."

"Shut up, Rachel! Just shut up!"

"That's enough," says Margaret. "Both of you."

"And I'm not sorry," says Jane. "But fine. Go on your stupid trip."

"What the devil is going on?" Wayne appears behind Jane and puts his strong arms over her shoulders.

Jane bursts into tears. "Nana's going to an island."

~

We all head to the garden to calm down.

Every day since we planted the bean seeds, Jane digs with her fingers in the dark garden soil, pulling out bean seeds, soft and splitting apart, sending out white, thread-like tendrils. She examines them and then gently pushes them back underground.

But today they've finally germinated—tiny green shoots lined up like happy campers in Margaret's garden.

~

After supper, Margaret, Jane, and I go to the Aspen Lake cemetery. Margaret's brought blue bachelor's buttons from her garden, and Jane has pussy willows. We put them in two glass jars with water on the gravestone where Mom's and Uncle Jimmy's ashes are buried. They're together because they were twins.

We sit on the memorial bench beside their gravestone. Last summer, Jane chose the words engraved on the back: *They loved each other.*

Jane wanders off to look for more Bird graves. The cemetery is full of our ancestors. I stay with Margaret.

This is the hardest part for Margaret. The cemetery.

# CHAPTER NINETEEN

On Sunday nights, Margaret sets up Wayne's pills in two long, plastic boxes, pink for the morning and yellow for the evening. Each box is divided into seven compartments, labeled with the days of the week.

Tonight, I'm helping. We slide pills out of their little bottles onto the kitchen table. Blue, green, yellow, white. Blood pressure, heart, cholesterol, gout, arthritis. Modern medicine has got Wayne covered. We count the pills carefully, five pills for each day, drop them into their compartments, and snap the lids down tight.

"He insists on keeping the pills in his room," says Margaret. "You'll have to remind him to take them. Once these boxes are filled, he has a fit if I touch them. He's terribly independent."

"Big surprise."

"You've got this silly blood pressure cuff to deal with, too."

"Don't worry."

Wayne doesn't cooperate? The kitchen goes on strike.

~

The week has flown by. Margaret's leaving tomorrow. She's in cleaning mode, vacuuming, dusting, tidying, discarding, sorting. When she picks me up at the store after school, she has a grocery list, things we already have lots of like Rice Krispies, milk, eggs, pasta, cocoa. Jane's with her and is allowed to pick out two treats.

"Oreos and Rocky Road ice cream! Please, please, please!"

While Jane's in the cookie aisle, Margaret chats with Peggy, and I check our mailbox. Nothing. No postcards. No SASEs.

"We should get going." Margaret stares at Jane. "What's all this?"

Jane's carrying a big bag of marshmallows and a box of graham wafers. "For s'mores," she says. "I just need to get a chocolate bar."

"Like s'mores are going to happen," I say. "News alert. There's a campfire ban. How are you going to roast the marshmallows?"

Jane sticks out her chin. Margaret sighs. "Put the graham wafers back. No chocolate. But we'll get the marshmallows. You can have one in your cocoa at night."

I carry boxes of food out to the truck. The Birds are ready for a siege. The enemy can barricade our fence line, but they won't starve us out.

When we get home, Margaret thinks she needs to rearrange the kitchen cupboards. "It'll make it easier for you to find things. Jane, take all the cans out of here and put them on the counter."

Jane loves this job. She's making high, wobbly towers. I scan the kitchen, which is rapidly turning into chaos. After tomorrow, I'll be in charge of all this. This is the first time it really sinks in.

~

We're picking at Margaret's shepherd's pie. No one's hungry.

"Why are you using the oven when it's so hot?" says Wayne. He's grumpy. Martin took him to a café in Lone Butte for lunch. That's a long day out for Wayne. He was driving Margaret crazy while she was packing, and she ordered him out of the house.

"I shouldn't be going away during a heat dome," says Margaret.

"It's not a heat dome yet," I point out. "It's just hot."

"You'll have to water the seedlings twice a day, Rachel. You'll need to put shade cloth on the lettuce in the afternoon or else they'll bolt. Maybe I—"

"How was lunch with Martin?" I say to Wayne.

"The girl waiting on our table had tattoos. All over her arms," says Wayne. "She's Bob Little's granddaughter."

Bob Little is one of his old cronies.

"Bob said she's moved up from the coast because she hates her parents. Her name's Ocean or Wave or something god-awful like that. Why don't people give their children normal names?"

"Because people don't want to be called Daphne anymore," I say.

"Now you listen to me, girlie. You should be damn proud of that name."

Daphne is my middle name, and I always hated it until I found out that I was named after my great-great-grandmother. Now I like it, but I'm not telling Wayne.

"I think those are interesting names," says Margaret. "Strong names for a girl." She smiles at me. "Daphne, too."

"And my name," pipes up Jane. "Jane Mary Bird. That's a strong name."

"What I was trying to say," says Wayne, "if people would stop interrupting me, is that the tattoos were appalling."

"Tattoos on young girls make them look so cheap," says Margaret.

Jane's eyes are bright. "What does that mean, cheap?"

"It means they look trashy," says Wayne. "Tattoos are for bikers. And convicts."

"And sailors," says Margaret.

She and Wayne are united on this.

"I like my tattoo." Jane displays a grubby splotch that used to look like a turquoise cat, just above her knee. "It looks good."

"And it also washes off," Margaret reminds her.

"Bob says the girl's parents have no control over her at all," says Wayne. "They should have forbidden her to plaster herself with tattoos."

I don't tell him that it wouldn't have worked. The Ministry of Health recommends that tattoo shops obtain prior parental consent if you're under the age of nineteen. Recommends. Not requires. I've made it a point to know this.

"That's the goddamn trouble with parents these days," Wayne steams on. "Everyone's afraid to say no to their kids. Afraid it will hurt their feelings. They want to be pals with their kids. When I was a teenager—"

I get up to clear our half-finished plates.

"Can we have ice cream?" says Jane. "And can I get a real tattoo?"

Wayne heaves himself to his feet. "Thank you very kindly for dinner, Margaret. And you listen, young lady."

Wayne never calls Jane girlie. That's just for me.

"A Bird with tattoos? Over my dead body."

# CHAPTER TWENTY

Jane and I load the dishwasher while Margaret and Wayne sit with their coffee. Wayne glances at the clock. "Put the radio on, Rachel. It's six."

I flip the dial on the radio on the shelf beside the sink. Music plays, then a woman's voice says that they're going to start the BC Wildfire Update. Wayne and Margaret listen to this twice a day.

The woman rambles through a whole list of places and numbers of acres that mean nothing to me. Then she says, "We will now update you on the current status of the Slack Lake fire, which has been burning since last Saturday."

Jane plunks down in Wayne's lap. "What—"

"Quiet, Jane," says Wayne. "I want to hear this."

"The fire advanced nine miles last night," says the woman. "Seventy-five thousand acres around Slack Lake have burned. The rural community of several hundred homes and summer cabins has been placed under an Evacuation Alert. However, no buildings are currently threatened. Two helicopters and twenty firefighters have been deployed to control the blaze."

Nine miles is the distance between us and the Aspen Lake store. A fire can go that far overnight? And seriously, two helicopters and twenty firefighters? How can that be enough?

"A change in wind direction this afternoon has caused the west flank of the Slack Lake fire to be more active," she says. "We are now classifying it as a fire of note."

She moves on to another fire somewhere else.

"What's 'fire of note' mean?" says Jane.

"It means they weren't paying attention to it before and they should have been," says Wayne. "You can thank our bloody prime minister for that. Turn it off, Rachel. I've heard enough. I need to take a look at this on a forestry map."

"I'm not going tomorrow," says Margaret.

"Of course you're going," he says.

He stumps off to his room, then comes back with a long paper roll. He spreads it on the table, smoothing it flat with his big hands. It's a maze of spidery black lines and lakes.

"Are we on here?" says Jane.

"You bet." Wayne puts his finger on the long narrow lake labeled Aspen Lake. "Our ranch is right here." Then he points to a small round lake. "That's Slack Lake. That's where they're talking about."

I study the map. "Are you really worried about this? It's so far away from us. The fire would have to cross the Thompson River first and then come all the way up the Big Hill."

"A fire can jump over a river?" says Jane.

"Oh, I don't think so," says Margaret.

"Damn right it can," says Wayne.

"What side exactly is the west flank?" I say.

"The side closest to us."

~

Jane and I google it.

*Fire of note: A wildfire that is highly visible or poses a potential threat to public safety.*

~

4 A.M.

"Hey, Rachel. Are you asleep?" Jane asks from my bedroom doorway.

"Yes."

"But how could—"

"Okay. No," I say. "But what are you doing in here?"

Jane sleeps in our uncles' old bedroom. I sleep in our mom's. Margaret's room is in between us.

"I need to tell you something."

Then she's beside my bed, and she stinks of pee. "Oh, Jane," I sigh.

I stagger out of bed and take her back to her room. We tiptoe so Margaret won't hear us. I whisk her out of her wet nightie and into a dry one.

"Don't cry," I say. "It's not a tragedy."

I can strip and change sheets at warp speed. I've had tons of practice. But not for a long time. Not since last fall.

"You can come back to my bed," I say. "But just this one time."

In my bed, Jane's bony elbow jabs my stomach, and I shift her over. "Okay, kiddo. What's going on?"

"I don't want Nana to go." Her skinny body shudders.

I squeeze her tight. "It's only for two weeks."

There's a long silence. I push her a little further away. Just in case.

"Rachel?" she mumbles.

"What?"

"Can I wear your ring again?"

"No."

*The ring.* I need to deal with it. But not in the middle of the night.

"Please, please, please."

"For five minutes. I'm timing you."

~

Susan and Wayne are drinking coffee in the kitchen. Margaret's helping Jane hunt for something for show-and-tell. They finally come downstairs, Jane clutching a blue and yellow bird from Margaret's collection of glass birds.

"She promises she'll be careful. Right, Jane?" Margaret sounds exhausted. "Is that Lucy I hear barking? Where is she?"

"Oops. I think I left her shut up in the garden," I say. "I'll get her."

"It's almost six-thirty," says Susan. "We were going to leave at six."

When I get back with Lucy, Jane says, "What's wrong with Bella?"

Bella's flopped down in the corner of the kitchen, chin on the floor, while Lucy sniffs Margaret's suitcase.

"She's depressed," I say.

"I'm going to stop taking that new pill," says Wayne. "It's giving me side effects."

"Oh my, I think I better—" says Margaret.

"Wayne Bird," bursts Susan. "Do you want us to miss that ferry? Margaret, go and get in the car. Right now."

"I'm just saying," says Wayne. "My head feels strange."

~

Jane's kicking dirt on the driveway with her running shoe. They just drove away, Susan honking the horn until her blue car disappeared around a bend.

"I'm going back to bed," mutters Wayne.

Jane and I go inside, and I pour two bowls of Rice Krispies. We take them outside to the verandah and eat our cereal sitting on the floor inside the Butterfly House. It's a little glass house at the end of the verandah. A long time ago, Margaret started seeds in here, but then Mom filled it with her origami butterflies. The butterflies hang from fine threads, twirling when you blow on them, a rainbow of colors. We always feel happy when we're in here.

"Who wants to go to school today?" I say. "Let's take a vote."

"Not me," says Jane.

"Not me," I say.

# CHAPTER TWENTY-ONE

I call Amber and tell her we're taking a mental health day and don't need rides. Then I saddle Magic and Dixie. We follow a trail that steadily descends through a part of the forest where the trees are close together. It's shady with moss-covered boulders and carpets of small white flowers that look like stars. It's good bone-hunting territory.

Jane's alert and finally spots a smooth flat bone, bleached white, in the grass. I tie it on the back of my saddle, while she walks around, kicking at the ground, because where there's one bone, there's sometimes more. Not today.

We get back on our horses, and soon we can glimpse the marsh through the trees. We come out by the old Bird homestead. The house, with its blackened logs and gaping shingle roof, has sunk even deeper into the grass than last summer. Swallows are swooping through the open windows where the glass broke years ago, repairing old mud nests and building new ones in the rafters.

We hook Magic and Dixie's reins to their saddles so they can graze and make our way carefully through nettles to the front of the house.

There's no door, just a splintered sill. I follow Jane inside. The floor is made of packed dirt and broken floorboards, splattered with bird shit. Shards of broken glass are everywhere.

Our great-great-grandparents Daryl and Daphne Bird built this house over a hundred years ago. Wayne's father, my great-grandfather, Joseph Bird, was born here, and Wayne was born here, too. Layers of history. All they left behind is an old black woodstove, a row of cupboards with peeling blue paint, and a piece of curtain nailed beside the window in one of the little bedrooms upstairs.

It's just a scrap of dirty cloth, cream-colored with pink roses. Who sewed those curtains? My great-great-grandmother Daphne or my great-grandmother Mary? Both of them lived in this house. Those curtains might have been the only pretty things they had.

We're forbidden to go up the stairs because Wayne thinks they're rotten and could collapse. We do anyway.

Jane scampers up the narrow wooden staircase. Her boots thud on the boards above my head. She's in the bedroom with the scrap of curtain. Nothing has changed since Mom played here with her friend. There's an old mattress and sleeping bag, a tea set on top of a wooden box, a yellow crate of books, a tin chocolate box with horses on the lid.

Mom wasn't allowed to go up the stairs, either. Mom, Jane, and me. This little room is our secret.

Jane likes to play with Mom's stuff. But I stay downstairs because if I go up there, I get very melancholy. I prefer poking around in the rubble, looking for stuff. More layers of history. All my discoveries are arranged on the woodstove—a whole collection of grimy bottles, a pot, a cracked blue teapot, an old-fashioned black shoe with the heel gnawed away, a leather belt, a tarnished fork.

I pick up the tall brown bottle, wipe the dust off with the edge of my T-shirt, and call up the stairs, "Bring me a piece of paper and a pencil, Jane!"

She's down in a second with a piece of the lavender paper from the tin box and a stub of a pencil. "What are we going to do?"

"We're making a layer of history."

I put the paper on top of the stove. I print in big block letters:

JANE MARY BIRD AND RACHEL DAPHNE BIRD WERE HERE.

Then I add the date and my signature. I get Jane to print hers, too. I roll the paper up tightly and slide it into the bottle. "Look for a good hiding place," I say.

Jane decides on a dark space under a floorboard in the back corner. She kneels and pushes the bottle in with a stick.

"Someone will find it in a hundred years," I say. "They'll be putting down a new floor and they'll find our bottle and they'll say, 'Well, what do you know? Look at this!'"

"They'll think it's a treasure map," says Jane.

"Maybe. And then they'll read it and say, 'I wonder who Jane Mary Bird and Rachel Daphne Bird were?'" I brush dirt off her knees. "Ready to go home now, kiddo?"

"Okay."

We ride back on an old tractor road. It follows a split-rail fence all the way to the barn. No one's driven a tractor on it for a few years and it's grown in with long grass and young aspen saplings.

As we leave the old house, I take one last look back. I always think I'll see a ghost at the little window tucked under the roof. A tall woman in an old-fashioned dress, cream-colored with pink roses.

~

"Do you remember what it was like when Nana was in the hospital?" I ask.

Jane's flopped on the kitchen floor beside Lucy. "Yes," she says warily. "I cried a lot. But Nana's not sick this time. She's having a holiday."

"That's true. She's not sick. But do you remember what the house was like?"

"Mega messy."

"Not mega messy. Just a bit—"

"I had to wear dirty clothes to school."

"Well, not every—"

"And the food you made was awful." Jane sits up. She's just getting started. "You made way too many scrambled eggs. Papa said so, too."

"Okay. Never mind that. This time, it's going to be different. Come here and sit down."

Jane plunks down beside me at the table. I slide a piece of paper in front of her. "Ta-da!"

"What's this?" she says.

"Your chore list."

She studies the paper in silence. She can't fake illiteracy because I taught her to read when she was three.

**JANE'S CHORES**

**Make your bed**
**Feed Lucy and Bella**
**Set the table for dinner**
**Unload the dishwasher**

**Put your dirty clothes in the laundry hamper**
**Pick up your toys**
**Brush your teeth without being asked**

"I have to do all this?" she says.

"Yup."

"Can I cook dinner instead?"

"No."

"What are you going to be doing?"

"Everything else."

~

Margaret calls. She's arrived. We put her on speaker. She has a lymph drainage treatment booked for tomorrow morning. Reiki in the afternoon.

"Do you have a TV in your house?" says Jane.

"It's a cabin," says Margaret. "No TV."

"Can you make sandcastles on the beach?"

"No sand. There's just little rocks and pebbles. But the waves make a lovely sound."

"When are you coming home?"

"Fourteen sleeps."

# CHAPTER TWENTY-TWO

Just before I go to bed, I check on Jane. She's moved from her top bunk to the bottom. Her sheet's crumpled around her feet. She's wearing Hoodie. Hoodie was Mom's. It's a red Roots hoodie that Jane slept in every night for a year after Mom died. Jane's small for her age, and she was lost inside it. She said it smelled like Mom. When Aleksandra tried to wash it, she screamed.

Jane's grown since the last time she wore Hoodie, but it still swallows her up. It's way too hot to be wearing it. There are beads of sweat on her forehead. I open her window wider, then shut the door quietly behind me. I check on Wayne next. He's puttering around in the kitchen.

"What are you doing?" I say.

"I was putting up a calendar for Jane to mark the days," he says. "Now I'm looking for the Ovaltine."

Wayne's taken the page for June from the calendar that comes with his Western Horseman subscription and tacked it to the kitchen wall.

"I'll make the Ovaltine," I say. "But first I'm taking your blood pressure."

"There's nothing wrong with my blood pressure," he says. "I have excellent blood pressure."

147 over 83.

*Not so good.*

And Margaret's only been gone for sixteen hours.

~

My phone dings. Text message from Harjit. She says, Check this out with a link.

It's a high school exchange site. I open it and up pops a picture of four girls taking a selfie in front of the Eiffel Tower. They're laughing, their arms draped around each other's shoulders.

STUDY IN FRANCE!

Are you a Canadian high school student seeking adventure?

Become an exchange student at an English-speaking high school in Paris!

Live with a French host family for a term, a semester, or a full school year.

Discover the real France!

I read through everything, feeling myself getting excited. I look at the criteria:

*Students must be between the ages of 15 and 19.* Check.

*Interested in learning about French culture and a desire to totally immerse yourself in the French language.* Check.

*Willingness to integrate into a French family.* Integrating into a new family? I'm a pro.

Then I look at the fees, and my heart sinks. Room and board are provided but there's no way Wayne and Margaret can afford those fees. It's thousands of dollars. Even if they could afford it, they wouldn't want to spend the money on this.

I skip to the next line.

*Financial assistance. Scholarships and bursaries are available to eligible applicants.*

Okay. I'm still alive. What would Aura, world traveler, say? She'd say, *Go for it.* I type in my name, age, the name of our high school, and my email. My finger hovers over the send button.

What will Cody say? I want him to like the idea, but he won't. He's never very interested in Aura's postcards. If I talk too much about Paris, he rolls his eyes. I think he'd be happy to stay in Aspen Lake his whole life. This place is in his blood. As far as he's concerned, Paris could be on the moon.

And Jane? We were all afraid to tell her that Margaret was going away for two weeks. How would I ever break this news to her?

*Application deadline: July 31.*

I look at the girls in the selfie again. That could be me.

I press send.

Then I climb into bed with *Lonely Planet: Pocket Paris.*

~

Amber and I have been riding for an hour, searching for her dad's cows. She rode over to our ranch this morning on Champion, Cassie perched behind on her saddle. The girls are with Wayne now, sorting

Jane's bones on the verandah. I left them with a plate of cookies and lemonade.

Some of Martin's cows are hanging out along the sides of the gravel road where there's still green grass in the ditches, others are grazing among the trees in the forest. The High Valley Ranch grazing license covers hundreds of acres of range land, so no one freaks out if cows disappear for a while. But now Martin's worried about water.

We ride along a trail through an area littered with dead trees, criss-crossed on the ground like pick-up sticks. More pine beetle kill. The grass is brown, and the wildflowers are pale and parched. Flies have found us, and Magic and Champion swish their tails.

We stop beside a hollow of dry, cracked black mud, the edges rimmed with white stuff that looks like chalk. It's the third dried-up pond we've seen today.

Amber jumps down off Champion and hands me his reins.

"The cows have definitely been here," she says, pointing to hoof-prints gouged in the hard mud. "But not for a while. Those are old tracks."

She swings back into her saddle.

"What's your dad going to do?" I ask.

"I dunno. He's talking about rounding up all the cows and bringing them home. Any stray ones left out here might find their way down to the lake over on the far side." She sighs. "Problem is, the terrain's pretty steep over there, not exactly easy for cows."

"Is he worried about this Slack Lake fire?"

"Super worried. Wayne?"

I think about Wayne's book and how he's obsessed with our family's history. He'd die if anything happened to our ranch. There's nowhere else in the world he could live.

"He doesn't talk about it much," I say, "but he's glued to the news and weather reports, and yeah, I'd say he's scared stiff. Me, too."

"It's so freaking awful." Amber wipes the sweat off her forehead. "Is every summer going to be like this from now on?"

I stroke Magic's neck and his ears swivel back.

"Climate change," I say.

~

Magic stands like a statue beside the pump house while I pour cool water from a hose over his back and sides. When I turn the hose off, he's dripping. I run a shedding blade across his black coat, careful to go the same way as his hair and to miss his hip bones. The blade pushes the water off his body in sheets, partly drying him. He drops his head and his lips wobble.

I spray him lightly with fly spray and slide his black-net fly mask over his ears and face. He's Darth Vader. Scary-looking but really a big softy. I take him to the field with a loose lead rope over his neck and let him go.

Three steps. He stops, folds his knees. *Ooomph.* He's down. He rolls and rolls, legs flailing in the air. A huge grunt and he heaves himself up and gives a shake. His still-damp coat is covered with dirt and dry grass.

Dancer whinnies, and Magic gallops away to join his buddies. Horses establish their hierarchy. After that, they're part of the herd. It's easy. They know how to fit in.

~

Amber's still here talking to Wayne by the hitching post while Champion waits patiently, flicking his tail at flies. Wayne's known Amber since she was a baby. She doesn't take any of his bullshit, and they can get into horrible arguments, but they really like each other.

I look around. "Where are the girls?"

"Making more lemonade," says Wayne.

That sounds scary. "I'll get them," I say.

Amber tightens Champion's girth. "Tell Cassie to hurry. I'm running late."

The lemonade jug is on the kitchen table, surrounded by lemons and a sea of white sugar that's spilled out of a tipped over paper sack. Jane's standing on a chair, reaching into a cupboard. She spins around, holding the bag of marshmallows.

"What are you doing?" I say.

"We didn't know how to cut the lemons," says Cassie.

"Jane?" I say.

She makes her eyes round. "I'm just *showing* Cassie the marshmallows."

I sigh. Choose your battles. "You can have one marshmallow each. Cassie, you gotta go. Jane, you can clean up this mess."

Jane hops off the chair. "Two marshmallows!"

"One. Don't push your luck."

~

Jane adores her calendar. She draws a red happy face for today's square.

"Twelve sleeps till Nana comes home," she says.

# CHAPTER TWENTY-THREE

Breakfast. I made a triple batch of pancakes last night that I heat up in the microwave.

Wayne and Jane are still in pajamas. I'm keeping one eye on the clock. I'm leaving first. I've got half an hour before Amber picks me up. Martin's taking Jane and Cassie to their bus stop later. I run through my mental checklist—before I go, get Jane dressed, find her show-and-tell, make her lunch.

I grab the maple syrup bottle from Jane. "Eat faster."

Wayne's watching the clock, too. "Put the radio on, Rachel."

BC Fire Updates. This morning they go right to the Slack Lake fire.

"Eight properties on the Turnpike Road are now under an Evacuation Order." It's the annoying man who's usually just on at night. "These are recreational properties, and several of the owners are refusing to leave. We're in communication with one of the owners at this moment."

The radio crackles. A gruff man's voice says, "This cabin's belonged to three generations of my family. I have a right to defend my property."

"Damn right you do." Wayne puts his fork down.

"Sir, a decision like this endangers our firefighters—"

"Then get us some help in here! I haven't seen a helicopter all morning. If you—"

"Unfortunately, we've lost our connection...the current number of acres burned is 150,000. The western flank continues to be very active. BC Forestry is asking all citizens to cooperate—"

"And watch our homes burn up," says Wayne.

"We will now update you on the Pine Canyon fire near Quesnel."

"Those poor buggers." Wayne pushes his chair back from the table. "I've heard enough."

~

Cody's staying in town after school. We always sit together on the bus. The trip goes faster when he's here, but I've got new library books in my backpack. Cody gets car sick if he reads on the bus, but not me.

I slide into our usual seat three quarters of the way down, right over to the window, and dig around in my backpack. I pull out: *A Storm of Swords* by George Martin, *Siege and Storm* by Leigh Bardugo, *Stormbird* by Conn Iggulden, and *Storm Glass* by Maria Snyder.

I love that moment of deciding which one to start first.

The bus stops and starts, dropping kids off, all the way to the Aspen Lake store. That takes over an hour. It's always super noisy, but I can block it out once I put earbuds in. But Sarah told me that was very unsociable. It's rude enough pulling out a book, but earbuds, too?

I pick *A Storm of Swords* and leave the other books on the seat beside me. I read two chapters in bliss, trying to shut out the noise all around me.

I'm briefly distracted when a whiff of cigarette smoke drifts up from the very back of the bus. One of the Lone Butte kids. No one from Aspen Lake smokes.

Our bus driver, Mr. Derwin, yells, "Put that out now or get off!"

Someone calls out, "Got it, Mr. Derwin!"

Every once in a while, I resurface. Check to see where we are. The bus pulls over in front of Dai's family's Vietnamese restaurant, at the side of the highway, and Dai hops off. That means we'll be at the store in fifteen minutes. I find myself listening unwillingly to Sarah and Tyson. They're directly behind me, across the aisle from each other, arguing about whether sour and sweet can be called tastes.

"Taste is like chocolate or mint or vanilla," says Tyson. "Sour and sweet are feelings on your tongue. They're not tastes."

"That's bullshit," says Sarah. "The five basic tastes are sweet, sour, salty, bitter, and savory. You learn that in Grade Three science."

"Then what's chocolate?" says Tyson. "I don't get that. And what the hell is savory?"

I turn around and say, "The savory taste is called umami. It was discovered by the Japanese."

They both stare at me. I shrug. "I read it in a book."

One more stop at a gravel road that goes to three resorts. Four kids get off. It takes Mr. Derwin a long time to pull back onto the highway. There's way more traffic than usual. Car after car and lots of pickups pulling trailers.

"What's going on, Mr. Derwin?" calls Tyson.

"It's all the people evacuating from Slack Lake," he says. "The highway's been busy all day."

Emma waits until the bus gets going again, then scoots up the aisle in a half crouch because Mr. Derwin goes ballistic if you stand up while the bus is moving.

He roars her name now. "Emma!"

"Sorry, Mr. Derwin." She scoops up my books and plops down beside me. "Are you still reading?"

I close *A Storm of Swords.*

"Today is Monday, right?" she says.

"Right."

"And I'm wearing my green sweater, right?"

"Right."

"I just realized something. I always wear my green sweater on Mondays. I don't think I even think about it. I just put my green sweater on. I'm not even conscience I'm doing it. It's freaking me out. Why do you think I do that?"

Emma's being super friendly. I try to focus. "Um…no idea."

I wish I had time to think about things like this. I glance out the window. We're just passing the community hall. Five minutes. I start my mental list of everything I have to do when I get home. The garden. The horses. Laundry is already piling up. And what am I going to make for dinner?

"Hey," says Emma. "Did you know that all your books have the word storm in the title? Whoa. That's even freakier than my green sweater. Maybe this is some kind of weird equinox year or something."

I burst out laughing. Emma's so crazy. I cram all my books back into my backpack. The rest of the way, we talk about all the things we want to do this summer. Before I know it, we're at the store.

~

I check our mailbox. One lone, white envelope, neatly addressed by me to Wayne. This is the last SASE I sent out. I fold it in half and slide it in my pocket. I hop into Amber's car.

"Hey, Amber."

"Hey, kiddo." She pulls out onto the highway. "Jane's at our place. She and Cassie are building a blanket fort in Cassie's room. Dad's watching them."

"When will Susan get back?"

"Tomorrow. I can keep Jane for dinner if you like."

Amber's been working from home this week. No Susan, they've got Wi-Fi problems.

"Thanks, but no. She should come home."

A red pickup passes us, towing a flatbed piled up with chairs, a couch, and boxes, secured with wide black straps. Then two trailers and a truck and camper.

"Evacuees from Slack Lake, I bet," says Amber. "I can't imagine what that would be like."

"What would you even take?" I ask.

A small car towing a boat crawls by, holding up four cars behind him. Amber honks in solidarity. Then she says, "How are things going with your friends?"

"Okay."

"Just okay? How's Sarah these days?"

"Fine. But I still think she resents me. I don't know why."

"Maybe she's jealous," says Amber.

"I doubt that."

"You gotta remember, to Aspen Lake kids, Vancouver is the big lights. She probably thinks you had a glamorous life there. I think she could be jealous. Lots of kids here can't wait to get to the city."

"Not Cody," I say. "He thinks only idiots want to live in a place like Vancouver."

Amber laughs. "Well, Cody is Cody. But don't pull away from everyone, Rach, just because you think you're different. Of course you're different. You didn't grow up in Aspen Lake. But who cares? When you get right down to it, we're all different. Just don't try to change. Okay? Be unique."

"Yeah, you're right," I say, "but it's hard."

"I know. And that's the end of my free advice. I've always been better at managing other people's lives than my own!"

We're at the gravel road. We switch places.

"One more thing," says Amber. "You snapped up the high school rodeo star. What's not to be jealous of?"

~

*Dear Mr. Bird,*

*Thank you very much for your query for* A History of a Pioneering Family: The Birds.

*We regret that we are not taking on any new authors at this time.*

*One suggestion. An interesting, catchy title will grab a reader. Maybe give that some thought.*

*Sincerely,*

*John Grander*

*Editor*

*Heron Book Publishers*

~

"Jane's class is having a year-end picnic on Friday, and she needs cupcakes," I say into the phone. "Enough for the whole class!"

"I should be there," says Margaret.

"No, you shouldn't," I say.

There's a pause. "Okay, pick up two cake mixes at the store."

"She wants pink icing."

"You can buy the icing there, too. It comes in little tubs. Get white and some red food coloring. That'll work."

"She's talking about sprinkles," I say.

"Jane can live without sprinkles," says Margaret.

"How did the hemp and sea salt scrub go?"

Margaret told me and Jane last night that she'd signed up for it.

"It was divine."

"What's next?"

"Sunrise meditation."

~

I tuck Jane into bed.

"Ten sleeps till Nana comes home," she says.

# CHAPTER TWENTY-FOUR

Cassie leaps out of the bus, but Jane steps down carefully, cradling her backpack tight against her stomach. Edna, the bus driver, taps her horn, makes a dusty U-turn, and leaves.

Jane sets her backpack on the ground. She opens the back door of the truck, picks up the backpack, and places it carefully on the seat. She climbs in.

"Aren't you going to say goodbye to Cassie?" I ask.

"Goodbye, Cassie!" she yells, then shuts the door.

Susan leaves first. Her car shoots up clouds of dust, so I wait a few minutes, then we head off, too.

"What?" says Jane.

"I didn't say anything."

I ease the truck over a part of the road that's like a washboard.

"What's in your backpack?" I ask.

"Nothing," says Jane.

"Why are you sitting in the backseat?"

"Because I want to."

"How was your day?"

"Good."

"How was the movie?"

"Good."

When we get home, Jane marches up to the house, her backpack pressed again to her stomach. She sweeps right through the mud-room and the kitchen, past Wayne who's eating leftover pancakes at the table. I block her exit to the stairs. "Where are you taking your backpack?"

"My room."

"On the table. Empty it. Now."

"O-kaaay." She makes a big show of pulling out some crumpled-up papers.

"Everything."

She sighs, reaches into the backpack, and slides out a pile of dirty, orange fur.

God. Another roadkill. Then the pile of fur moves up and down. It's breathing. Just barely. It has two ears, one torn off at the end, the other mostly skin with no fur. It has two very sticky eyes, three quarters shut. I can't tell if it has a tail.

"It's a cat." Jane's voice rises. "He's starving. I found it at school. Can I keep him, Papa? Please, please, please."

A yucky, smoky smell is wafting around the laundry room. "He stinks," I say.

Wayne puts down his fork. He probes the cat gently with his big hands. "Some of his fur is singed. He's been near a fire. Where exactly did you find him, Jane?"

"Under the portable behind the school. Me and Cassie heard him crying."

He's not crying now, I think. More like dying.

"He could have jumped out of a car leaving Slack Lake," says Wayne.

A forest fire evacuee. I look at the cat with more respect.

"Please, please, please," says Jane.

"I don't know." Wayne's not crazy about cats. Neither is Margaret. They kill the birds in her garden.

"He's starving." Jane's not giving up.

"Just don't let Lucy and Bella near him," says Wayne finally. "That cat's got lice."

"Tell me it's not the same kind of lice that people get," I say.

~

"Marmalade," I say. "Or Ginger."

"I already named him," says Jane. "He's Mr. Boney."

We're in the laundry room, about to give the cat a bath in dog shampoo called Skunk Off. Mr. Boney is going to live in the laundry room. That's my executive decision.

"Rubber gloves." I'm digging in the drawer by the washing machine. "He could be contagious."

I lower Mr. Boney into the sink. He slumps onto his belly, legs splayed. We massage the shampoo into his filthy fur. The smell of smoke mixed with wet fur is nauseating. The singed bits are horrible. I peek into matted clumps. I'm trying unsuccessfully to confirm that Mr. Boney really is a *he*. How do you even tell with a cat?

"He's so gentle. Don't you think he's gentle, Rachel?" says Jane.

"Mmmm."

"He's getting way orangier," she says.

There's white in there, too. I get a piece of paper towel, soak it in clean, warm water, and wipe off the mucus-y, yellow gunk around his eyes. They slant open and stare at us. Slits of green ice.

Jane's fallen in love. We dry Mr. Boney with a blow-dryer while his frosty eyes stare into space. They're getting gooey again, and I give him another paper towel treatment. I get some nail scissors, and we try to snip away some of the mats.

Jane makes a bed out of old towels in the corner of the laundry room. We tuck Mr. Boney into his nest. Jane sets out two saucers, one of milk and one of water. I find an old plastic bin that will do for now for a litter box. I send Jane outside for some sand and gravel from the driveway.

When she gets back, she says, "Mr. Boney's purring!"

"Actually, he's trying to breathe," I say. "He probably has asthma as well as lice. And remember, keep this door closed all the time. We don't want the dogs in here. You heard Papa."

"Mr. Boney has to stay in here forever?" says Jane.

"Until he gets better."

This is what I'm really thinking: This is one sick cat. He'll be dead by dinnertime.

~

Mr. Boney isn't dead by dinner time.

"Can I sleep in the laundry room tonight?" says Jane.

"No," I say.

"Can I eat dinner in the laundry room?"

"No."

"Papa, can I eat dinner in the laundry room?"

When it comes to Jane, Wayne always caves. "I don't see why not."

~

I open my inbox. Still nothing from the Paris exchange program. For the hundredth time, I check the *Sent* box to make sure my email went. It did.

I was too late. They've already got everybody.

~

"Let's think about a new title for your book," I say. We're at the kitchen table, eating Rice Krispies for breakfast.

"What?" says Wayne.

"A new title."

"Why?"

"Something on a bird theme," I say. "Interesting and catchy. Like...'Feather Your Nest.'"

Wayne stares at me. I grab the sugar bowl away from Jane. "'As the Crow Flies' would be good."

"'The Early Bird Gets the Worm!'" says Jane.

It takes Wayne, huffing, almost a whole minute to heave himself out of his chair.

"Wayne, are you taking your pills every—"

Outside, Amber honks her horn.

She's early or I'm late. Wayne vanishes, and Jane scampers upstairs. As I wrap up three pancakes to put in her lunch kit, I come up with the best title yet: "Free Like a Bird."

Amber honks again. I shout up the stairs, "Susan will be here in forty minutes. Are you listening, Jane? Get a T-shirt out of the basket with clean clothes, not dirty ones! I'm going now!"

This is the one day I absolutely have to get to town.

# CHAPTER TWENTY-FIVE

I push open the door of Spiderweb Tattoos, hidden away on a backstreet.

Lannie, the receptionist, beams at me from behind a counter. Duke, the tattoo artist, is the owner. Lannie's his sister. "Hey! Wow! Cool! Duke and I had a bet. I said you wouldn't show."

My smile feels tight. Lannie has turquoise hair, studs in her lips. No tattoos. Should that tell me something?

"Duke'll be five," she says. "He's finishing up his coffee break."

"Okay."

"You seemed kind of freaked out when you came by last week."

"Me? Not at all."

I wander around, wondering why I'm here. The walls are covered with tattoo art. Most of it's fantasy stuff that I really love. Lots of dragons and snakes and skulls. But that's not what I'm getting.

"That's all Duke's work," calls out Lannie.

"It's impressive."

"So, how are ya feelin'?"

Doesn't she have something to type or file?

"Fine."

I perch on a plastic chair and take a piece of paper out of my backpack. Harjit went online and printed a list of questions you should ask before you get a tattoo.

*Are you a licensed tattoo artist?*

*How long have you been doing tattoos?*

*Can you tell me about the ingredients in the ink you use?*

*Do you sanitize your equipment?*

*Do you adhere to the safe disposal of blood and have gone through borne pathogen courses?*

I get up and look around again. It's all amazing. Parrots. A peacock with human eyes all over its fanned tail. Red roses twined together, dripping blood. A gorgeous blue and gold butterfly. It could be one of the butterflies in the Butterfly House.

Butterflies always make my heart miss a beat. Mom had a little butterfly tattoo between her shoulder blades. That's where my tattoo's going. Same place. I take a big breath.

Now I remember why I'm here.

~

Duke takes me into a little room with a couple of chairs and a massage bed. Except for his face, he's plastered with tattoos. I try to distract myself by studying the coiled-up snake on his shaved head instead of looking at all the stuff he's trying to explain: ink caps, needles, petroleum jelly, the tattoo machine that makes the needles vibrate as they go into your skin, antibacterial soap, gloves.

*Do you use latex-free gloves?*

I promised Harjit I'd ask, but I'm paralyzed. Why didn't I get Carlee to come with me? She'd have been perfect. She'd be firing questions at Duke. Taking notes. Or Cody. He could have held my hand. They don't even know I'm here. No one does.

I take off my shirt. I'm wearing my bikini top underneath because I knew I'd feel weird in a bra. I sit on one chair and lean forward onto another. My heart's racing five hundred miles an hour.

"*Draumstafir*?" says Duke.

"Yes," I whisper.

"My first," he says.

Did he mean draumstafir or tattoo?

*How long have you been doing tattoos?*

"Let's do this," says Duke.

~

It's not too bad. Prickly and stingy but nothing intense. It's a simple design, just a staff with swirly lines. Small, black and white except for a green vine wound around the staff. Duke hums while he works.

"That's it," he says after about an hour and a half. "You're gonna be happy. I'll put a bandage over it to keep it clean. You gotta wait a few days before you show all your friends, okay?"

"Okay. Thanks so much, Duke."

"My pleasure."

I follow him out to the main room. My turn to beam at Lannie. I love her now. A guy's standing at the counter. He turns around. "Rachel? What are you doing here?"

It's Owen, Sarah's older brother.

Shit.

"Research for an essay," I mumble.

"End of year assignment?"

"Something like that."

Lannie passes me some papers stapled together. "Your receipt's there and some information about aftercare." Does she have to shout? "You shouldn't have any problems, but remember to keep the bandage on for a day or two. And come right back if you think there's something wrong."

I look right past Owen and leave.

~

I'm going to hang around the bookstore until it's time for the bus.

"I was hoping you'd come in," says Harjit. "How'd it go?"

"Easy. I can't show you because I have to keep it covered for a few days."

"Of course." Harjit believes in rules. "You went with the draumstafir?"

"Yup."

"Now you'll have great dreams."

"That's the theory."

The draumstafir's a sleep symbol. I know about it because of Jesse. He has a tattoo of a Viking compass on his shoulder. He printed off some designs for me from something called the *Huld Manuscript*, and that's where I found the draumstafir.

Harjit gives me a half-hug, shoulders only.

Is my back supposed to feel like it's on fire?

"Harjit, how can I tell if I'm allergic to tattoo ink?"

~

Jane draws a purple happy face.

"Eight sleeps till Nana comes home," she says.

Eight sleeps. Margaret's going to hate my tattoo. As for Wayne… too scary to think about.

# CHAPTER TWENTY-SIX

Jane pulls a crumpled paper out of her backpack.

"What's that?" I ask. "Does Papa need to sign it?"

"Nope," she says. "It tells all about Canada's Food Guide. We had to take everything out of our lunch kit and spread it on our desk, and everyone had to say if it was healthy. And then we had to tell Mrs. Layton what we had for breakfast."

Mornings in this house are now a blur. Breakfast? When Margaret's in charge, Jane has oatmeal on school days and Rice Krispies on the weekend.

"So, what did you tell Mrs. Layton you had?"

"Rice Krispies. She made a face." Jane makes a face, too. "And I was supposed to have some fruit."

What did I pack in Jane's lunch kit this morning? A jam sandwich and Oreo cookies? I know I remembered an apple.

"Did she see your apple?"

"What apple?" says Jane. "We have to write everything we eat in our food journal. We're gonna do it all week. And Cassie says Oreos—"

"Cassie was pretty excited to eat Oreos last time she was here."

"Cassie says—"

"Forget Cassie. I've got a brilliant idea. You can pretend to be me. You can write down everything I eat. You'll be the star of Grade One."

~

Against my better judgment, Jane's gone with Wayne for his walk. Before they set out, I gave her strict instructions: Don't go past the pine tree. Come back right away if there are too many mosquitoes. *Don't run.*

While they're gone, I look for dirty clothes in Wayne's room. It's stuffy and it smells like Bella. There are rumpled sheets on his unmade bed, three coffee mugs beside a pile of books on the night table. I open the window, pick up some socks and pajamas from the floor, grab a plaid shirt hanging on his chair, and juggle two of the mugs. A final glance around and I spot the plastic pill box on his desk, on top of a stack of his ranching magazines.

I set my load down on a corner of the desk and snap open the lid of each little compartment. Pills in most of them and never the same ones. Two pills here, four pills there, a jumble of yellow, blue, red, and green. It's Thursday today. Monday still has all five pills, Saturday and Sunday are empty.

~

I'm at the kitchen window, watching Wayne and Jane come back. Wayne's striding along with his canes. He looks spry.

Call it a close call.

"The pillbox has moved to the kitchen counter," I say. "I'm your new gatekeeper."

We eye each other. It's a standoff.

Then he says, "I want to see this tattoo."

~

How did he know? He's psychic. And there's no way he's going to just let this go by without giving me grief. But I need him to look at my back because it feels awful. For all I know, I have a raging infection. I lay on the couch, face down, and slide up my T-shirt. I wince as Wayne pulls off the bandage.

"Oh my God!" says Jane.

"Is it infected?" I ask.

"It will be," says Wayne. "Jane, go look in Nana's bathroom. Bring any tubes of ointment that you can find."

I keep my face buried in a cushion.

Jane comes back with a stash of tubes, pink calamine lotion, toothpaste, hair conditioner, eye cream, and petroleum jelly.

"Ah," says Wayne, sorting through the pile. "Polysporin. This will do it."

He rubs the cream in gently. It's deliciously cool. I think I'll stay here forever.

"What's it supposed to be?" says Jane. "You can't even tell."

"I'll tell you later," I mumble. "I'd like to be alone for a while."

"We'll have some ice cream, Jane." Wayne sounds annoyingly cheerful.

"Just one thing," I say. "How did you know?"

"Duke called me."

"He called you?"

"He's an Aspen Lake kid," says Wayne. "I've known him since he was a baby. He used to toss hay bales for me."

"Oh."

"He was worried about your age. Sixteen, in case you've forgotten."

"Did he call you before or after I got the tattoo?"

"Before," says Wayne.

~

Jane and I are icing cupcakes. Happy faces are marching across the calendar. Seven sleeps till Margaret gets home. Halfway there.

# CHAPTER TWENTY-SEVEN

It's Mr. Boney's first supervised visit outside the laundry room.

Jane's holding a purple cat harness that Susan lent her, and I'm holding Mr. Boney, who's staring at me with his cold, green eyes. "I'm not doing this by myself," I say. "I'll keep a grip on him, and you put the harness on. And be careful."

Mr. Boney is thrashing back and forth in my arms. It's scary how much difference a few days of food can make. "Faster Jane," I say.

She's trying to figure out the harness. "Does his head go through here?"

We trade. Jane holds on tight. I push Mr. Boney's head through an opening, pull his front legs through another opening, and snap shut the buckle on his back. He lets out a long, throaty growl. I reach for the buckle under his tummy.

"Don't let go of him!" I say.

"Sorry!"

Mr. Boney tumbles in a heap to the floor.

"That doesn't look right," says Jane.

"Good enough," I say. "Let's get this over with."

~

Mr. Boney's huddled on the grass, his eyes shut.

"He won't move," says Jane.

"Pull harder," I say.

"I'm trying."

Mr. Boney rolls over on his back.

"Oh my God, Mr. Boney," says Jane.

The next part happens at warp speed. A fat, innocent robin lands on the grass, just out of Mr. Boney's reach. Even upside down with his eyes shut, his radar picks it up. He flips over, crouches, then pounces, yanking the leash out of Jane's hand.

She screams. Mr. Boney dives into the bushy part under the lilac, carrying his victim. I assess the situation, then send Jane to the house for oven mitts.

As I haul him out, his razor claws pierce through the mitts like tiny knives.

Mr. Boney's going back to solitary confinement.

~

Amber drops Cassie off to play with Jane. Cassie has her pink backpack, and Amber pours out instructions. "She's got sunscreen on and she's brought a sun hat and her bathing suit in case they want to play in the sprinkler—"

"Go," I say. Amber is a mother hen when it comes to Cassie. Maybe that's what happens when you're a single mom. Thank God I never had to test that theory.

Cassie is Mr. Boney's official aunty. She helped Jane rescue him from under the school portable. She knows a lot about cats.

"They like to play inside things," she says. "We should make him a house."

Wayne still has the cardboard box that his TV came in. I find some old poster paints, and the girls paint it like a rainbow. I remember seeing a roll of used carpet in the shed. I find it in a cobwebby corner behind a saggy mattress. I cut off a square with an X-Acto knife, and Cassie and Jane glue it into the bottom of the box.

"Cats like windows in their houses," says Cassie.

They use Jane's blunt-ended school scissors and gouge out one roundish, raggedy hole. I carry the box into the laundry room. Mr. Boney's buried in his towels. We can hear him chewing his fur.

"Hey!" says Jane.

Mr. Boney's head emerges from the towels. Jane crouches down. "We built you a house!"

He spits.

"Nice kitty," says Cassie.

"Should I put him inside now?" says Jane.

"That's the plan," I say.

"Like, right now?"

"I guess so."

Jane scoops Mr. Boney up in an armful of towels and drops him inside the box. He swipes at her with his paw but misses. There's a strange gargling sound deep in his throat.

"Cats like it when you close the box," says Cassie.

I close the flaps.

It's dead quiet.

"What are you doing in there, Mr. Boney?" says Jane.

Cassie kneels and peers in the window.

I grab her arm. "That's not a good—"

An orange paw blasts out through the hole. Cassie screams and tumbles onto her back.

"Shit!" I say. "Are you alright?"

"There's blood on your cheek!" says Jane. "It's pouring out!"

Cassie starts to sob. "Cats—"

"Stand back, both of you!" I pull open the flaps on the box, kick it over on its side, and jump away.

"Cats—" gasps Cassie.

An orange head pokes out through the flaps. I push the girls ahead of me and bang the door shut. "Go look for some Band-Aids, Jane. I'm going to make a sign for the door. 'Enter at your own risk.'"

"Ha, ha," says Jane. "Where will we do our laundry?"

"In the creek."

~

Jane and Cassie play in the hammock, and I go to the garden to weed. It's noon and the sun's right overhead. I'm praying that's why everything in here looks so droopy. One week and the garden has died?

I think Margaret said to only water in the morning and the evening, but I move the sprinkler beside the broccoli and cabbage plants and turn it on. Then I start weeding the carrots at the other end of the garden. It's hot, but cool water from the sprinkler lands like mist on my bare arms and legs.

I'm getting into a rhythm when Amber's back, honking her horn. I turn off the sprinkler, shout for Jane and Cassie, and grab my backpack from the mudroom. Amber's taking us all to the store: the girls for ice cream and me to meet up with Cody.

No girls.

Amber honks her horn again, but they still don't come. She unrolls her window, and I say, "They're playing in the hammock. I'll—"

That's when Jane screams.

~

Amber and I run. The girls are behind the old shed. I see everything in one horrified second—Cassie's pink backpack, the bag of marshmallows, and two metal roasting sticks from our firepit, all dumped in the gravelly dirt. Flames are soaring high above their heads.

Jane screams again.

"Oh my God!" says Amber. "What the hell are you doing?"

The girls are riveted on the fire. I grab their arms and yank them back. The flames keep climbing.

"Amber, get water!" I yell.

Shit. There's a dead pine tree twenty feet away. Sparks are blowing around. A piece of smoldering newspaper lands in a clump of dry grass. I stamp it out.

"Over here, Rachel!" yells Jane.

I stomp on another scrap of burning paper.

Then suddenly it's over. In a few seconds, the flames die down to nothing.

What just happened? I realize now that it was mostly newspaper burning. A pile of crumpled newspaper and some dry twigs.

"Are you out of your mind, Jane?" I say. "What were you thinking?"

"Cassie said we should do it!" she says.

"I did not!" Cassie screams.

"Yes, you did!" Jane screams back. She erupts into sobs.

Amber's back with a bucket sloshing water. "Oh, thank God," she says. "It's out."

I grab the bucket from her and pour the water over the pile of curled, black ashes. It turns into a soggy gray mess.

Then I spot a box of matches, near a stump, and pick them up. "Where did you get these?"

Jane's crying so hard now she can't talk.

I don't recognize the box. I try to keep my voice even. "Cassie, did you bring these matches?"

Cassie's face has turned almost white under her freckles but she's not crying. "No," she says.

"Yes, you did," Jane sobs. "In your backpack."

"Cassie," says Amber. "Did you bring the matches?"

Cassie bursts into tears.

"I'll take that as a yes." Amber grabs her arm. "You are in big trouble, young lady."

Cassie wails even louder.

"You didn't even check to see what was in her backpack, Amber?" I say.

That's totally unfair. I never look in Jane's backpack. She could march out of here with all our kitchen knives, for all I'd know. But I can't help it. I'm just so upset. "Cassie can sneak matches just like that?"

"No, I did not look in her backpack," says Amber. "And I don't like the word *sneak*, Rachel. Cassie doesn't sneak. And maybe Jane shouldn't be quite so quick to blame her friend. Maybe she should take some responsibility for herself for a change."

"For a change? What's that supposed to mean?"

The girls have stopped crying and are staring at us, eyes wide.

"Are you going to tell Papa?" says Jane.

~

The girls are in the backseat. They're not saying a word. Jane's probably wondering if she's still going to get ice cream. Or maybe she really is sorry. I have no clue anymore. I stare out the passenger window. Amber doesn't ask me to drive. Not that I want to. I'm still shaking.

I wipe away a tear that's trickling down my cheek, hoping she doesn't notice. She reaches her hand out and touches my arm. "Hey, kiddo. It's no one's fault. Not yours or mine. I was scared. I didn't mean what I said about Jane."

The last thing I want is to fight with Amber. "Me neither. About Cassie."

"Truce?"

I seem to be always making up with someone. "Truce."

I hardly ever talk about Jane's burn, but I think about it every time I see the puckered skin on her arm. And now it's getting all mixed up with this. Amber's wrong. It is my fault. I was in charge of the girls. They were playing in the hammock and then what? How long did I go without checking on them? I screwed up when Jane was three, and I screwed up today. So much for keeping her safe.

They could have burned the ranch down. Because that's how it happens. Except for a few ignorant pyromaniacs, no one means to start a forest fire. It's a stupid mistake. You hear it on the news. Someone drops a cigarette. Someone doesn't put out their campfire. Two little kids try to roast marshmallows.

That's how it happens.

# CHAPTER TWENTY-EIGHT

Cody's in a great mood. He just waterskied, barefoot, no skis, and he stayed up for ten minutes. No one does that.

"Way to go, dude. That was amazing," says Dai.

"You should've seen your face trying to get up. You were in pain," says Tyson, who still hasn't mastered slalom.

"It hurt like hell," says Cody. "Did you see how many times I almost wiped out? It was crazy."

Cody doesn't know how to boast. He doesn't need to. That's something I really love about him. He grabs a Coke out of a cooler of ice. He presses it against the back of my neck as he plunks down on the dock beside me.

"Hey! Quit it!" I slap his arm. "That's cold."

His thigh presses against mine. It feels nice. I've finally stopped thinking about Jane and Cassie's fire, and I'm starting to relax and have a good time. We're both watching Carlee, who just dove into the lake and is doing a strong front crawl to the raft. She pulls herself up. She has the longest legs ever. Waterdrops sparkle on her dark skin.

I'm obsessed with getting a tan. I glance down at Cody's legs. Golden with blond hairs. My feet, dangling in the water, look like two white fish.

"How come you're not waterskiing?" asks Cody.

"I don't know. Don't feel like it."

"So, what's with the T-shirt?"

I'm wearing a baggy purple T-shirt over my bikini. A tank top would've looked less obvious but my tank tops are tight and don't have high backs.

"Sunburn," I mumble.

"Right." He falls backward onto the bleached boards of the dock, legs still in the water. "Ouch! Burning back!" He gives an enormous sigh. "God, this feels good."

The sky is dark blue. It's super hot. Carlee's back, dripping water from her long hair on Cody's stomach. We're all chilling, and everyone—except me—is eating chips and drinking soda. I have my faithful water bottle and apple. A boat, way out on the lake, is pulling a screaming kid on a tube. Some guy's fishing at the point. This is the busy end of Aspen Lake. Our ranch is way down the other end where it's quiet, and better. But it's fun here.

Someone brings up the forest fire, but no one feels like talking about it. I think we're all getting sick of the subject. Carlee is the only one who really doesn't have to worry. Rocky Lake reserve is nowhere near any fire.

"If you get evacuated, you can all come stay with me," she says, joking. The fire isn't a joke, but we're all in that beginning-of-summer mood. Who wants to wreck that?

"Hey, Rachel," says Sarah. "Owen says he saw you at that tattoo place last week."

I'm trying to think how to answer that when Tyson says, "Are you getting a tattoo?"

"Uh...I was just...."

"You're getting a tattoo?" says Dai.

Everyone's staring at me, and *shit*, I know I'm turning bright red.

"Maybe she's already got the tattoo," says Sarah. "First clue: T-shirt."

Tyson, Dai, and Emma laugh. Cody doesn't. Carlee catches my eye, and she looks puzzled (we tell each other everything) but sympathetic. She's had some conflicts with Sarah this year.

"Okay," says Sarah. "Reveal all. Let's see it."

I don't know what else to do. I put my water bottle down, peel off my T-shirt, and turn around. No one says anything for at least three hours.

Then Tyson says, "What is it?"

"A draumstafir." Carlee remembers everything.

"What the hell's that?" he asks.

"An Icelandic magical stave," says Carlee.

Emma looks shocked. "Is it supposed to be puffy like that?"

"Of course, it's going to be puffy for a little while." Carlee smiles at me. "I think it's fantastic!"

"Wow," says Emma. "I love it. I really do, Rach."

"How much did it cost?" says Sarah, even though you can bet Owen told her.

Their questions swirl around me. I stumble out some answers.

Cody gets up.

He walks to the end of the dock and dives into the lake.

~

I put one more load of laundry in the washing machine and head out to the hammock with my book. I'm still fuming since yesterday. That was so immature of Cody. What does he expect? That I'm always going to ask his permission first for everything I want to do?

He didn't ask *me* about the ring. Just when everything was getting good again, he does this.

Instead of reading, I lie still. I'm not going to think about Cody right now. I'm going to admire Jane's sheets. They're billowing like sails on the clothesline, green with yellow polka dots, pale blue with floating white clouds and pink candy cane stripes. There are more sheets in the washing machine. I swing out of the hammock and head to the house to see if they're ready to hang up. Wayne's on the verandah, helping Jane with a jigsaw puzzle. She shoots me a look, but she doesn't need to worry. We made a deal. I won't tell Wayne about the fire, and she'll stop telling me what Cassie says and start thinking for herself.

"You're outside," I say to Wayne.

He glares at me. "I've been driven outside. How is a person supposed to write with all that banging and crashing going on? Do you have to wash everything in one day?"

Our temperamental washing machine is down a short hallway from Wayne's bedroom.

"I'm being efficient," I say. "This is laundry day."

"You listen to me, girlie. It's Sunday. I expect some peace on a Sunday morning. And by the way, I've asked Cody to come over this afternoon and take the horses' shoes off."

"What for?" I'm not ready to forgive Cody. And there's always the risk that he'll ask for the ring back. I do not want him here today.

"Their shoes could hit a rock and make a spark," says Wayne. "It's not going to be because of the Birds that Aspen Lake burns up." Jane looks terrified, but I keep my eyes on Wayne.

"We're not going to burn up," I say. "We're on the plateau. Margaret says she doesn't ever remember a forest fire near Aspen Lake. It's in the valleys that you have to worry."

I don't believe it. I'm not sure why, but I don't.

"You can't ride right now, anyway," says Wayne. "The horses will get all lathered up. It's bad for them. Now, have you finished washing things for today?"

"Still got all the towels."

He closes his eyes. "Next thing I know, you'll be running the well dry."

~

In the kitchen, I'm filling Wayne's pillbox for the week when Jane streaks in. "Something's wrong with the sun!"

I follow her out through the mudroom. The sun is a perfect, brilliant red circle in the hazy sky, like someone cut it out of red construction paper and stuck it there.

"Wow!" I say.

"Why is it red?" says Jane.

"It's gotta have something to do with all the fires. We better not stare at it."

"Will it burn our eyeballs?"

"Who knows? But let's not chance it."

"Maybe it's Mars," says Jane. "I just took one more peek. Mars is red."

"Nope. It's the sun," I say. "Weird, huh?"

"I think it's beautiful."

Jane's right.

It's disturbing, but it's beautiful.

We google it:

*Fire smoke contains billions of miniscule smoke particles, which can scatter the purple, blue, green, and yellow light and make the sun look bloodred, even in the middle of the day.*

"I don't see any smoke," says Jane.

"They're just tiny particles. Microscopic," I say. "That's because where the smoke's coming from is really far away."

"How far away?"

"The other side of a river."

~

Jane's talking to Margaret. When she gets off the phone, she says, "Nana says she wishes she saw the red sun. And she says to tell you that the shade cloth can stay on the lettuce all the time now and not just in the middle of the day."

The shade cloth. Shit. How could I have forgotten the shade cloth? When was the last time I even looked at the lettuce? When did I have time?

I go to the garden to inspect. Each lettuce plant has shot up into an almost ten-foot spikey thing. When did that happen? Overnight? How come I didn't see it before? I pick off a leaf, chew, and spit it out. Bitter.

The lettuce plants have bolted. That's another name for heatstroke. I learned that from Margaret. They look like they should be growing in the Amazonian jungle, not in her garden.

# CHAPTER TWENTY-NINE

"Come on, old guy," says Cody. "Give me a break."

He's holding up Magic's back left hoof, bracing it against his thigh on top of his leather apron. Magic's leaning all his weight into Cody, grunting. Swishing his tail. I'm standing at Magic's head, stroking his face. Cody has already finished Dancer and Dixie.

Magic's ears slant back. He's twenty-five and sometimes stiff in his hind end.

This is the last shoe. Cody's pried up the tops of the nails along the rim of Magic's hoof using a hammer and something that looks like a thick blade. He straightened the nails, so they'll slip through the hoof, and now he's working the shoe loose. He learned how to do all this from Jesse. He's really good at it.

He tosses the shoe in a bucket with a clatter. He'll pull the nails out later and reuse the shoes if they're not too worn down.

"Almost done, Magic." He rests Magic's hoof on an iron anvil and Magic's body shifts a little. "That feels better, huh?"

I've always loved how kind Cody is with Magic. Like he's got all the time in the world. He's like that with his own horses, too. I've never seen him get mad at a horse. He trims the edge of Magic's hoof with clippers and smooths it with a file. Then he picks up Magic's foot and places it gently on the ground.

"Good fellow." Cody stands up straight. There's a round circle of sweat on his T-shirt between his shoulders.

Magic wanders onto the strip of grass by the barn while I pick up the curved crescents of hoof trimmings. Jane gives them to Lucy and Bella.

"Thanks, Cody," I say.

"Yeah. No problem."

He takes off his leather apron, then stretches his back. "Dad said Wayne's gotta decide what you want to do with your horses if you have to evacuate. We can put all three of them in our horse trailer and take them out to Meadow Lake. But we can't leave it to the last minute. We got our own horses to think about, too."

While he's talking, he's walking around, picking up stray nails lying on the ground. He's super careful that way.

"Evacuate?" I say. "Who said anything about evacuating?"

"That Slack Lake fire could run right up the hill."

"It's on the other side of the Thompson River."

Cody shrugs. "Yeah, but it's doubled in size in three days. Anything could happen."

"That's pretty negative," I say.

"Maybe."

I see him glance at my hand, then look away. He does that a lot. Like he thinks that maybe the ring will suddenly appear. Presto! Or maybe I'm imagining it. Maybe I think he's looking at my finger and thinking about the ring, but he's really not.

"About yesterday," I say. "I didn't really appreciate what you did."

"And what did I do?" He puts his tools into a second bucket.

"Your big dramatic exit. Just walk away and dive in the lake. That wasn't cool."

"Yeah?" Cody looks straight at me.

"You didn't say anything to me," I say. "It was embarrassing in front of everyone."

"And how do you think I felt? You're supposed to be my girlfriend and I get to see the tattoo the same time as everyone else? You made me look like an idiot."

"That's ridiculous."

"To you, maybe," he says. "And you didn't even bother to tell me you were getting it. Nice."

"You knew I was getting a tattoo."

"*One* day. I didn't know you were going to do it last week. I should have gone with you."

"I don't like the *should*, Cody. I don't need you to hold my hand," I say, even though I know I thought it would have been nice if Cody *had* been there to hold my hand. But that's not the point.

Cody takes off his leather apron. He pushes his hair back from his sweaty face. "Whatever, Rachel," he says.

It's impossible to keep a fight going with Cody. It's infuriating. He just won't.

He sighs. "What do you want to do now?"

There's only one possible option on a day this hot. Swimming.

~

We take the trail that meanders through trees. The trees make you think it's shady even though the sun is barely visible in the gritty sky, and there is no shade. Everywhere is the same dullness. Dry sticks crack under our running shoes. The few wildflowers that have bloomed, scattered pockets of lupines, purple asters, and drooping tiger lilies, have dried up, their colors faded. No birdsong.

The lake matches the sky, flat and gray. Our two canoes, mine and my mom's old orange one, are flipped over and leaning against the bank. Margaret calls this the beach. Grass, the smooth tops of rocks sticking out of the water, water lilies, a half-submerged fallen tree. Not really a beach but you can swim here.

"Island?" asks Cody.

"It's way too hot to paddle," I say. "Let's just swim here."

We sit on the bank side by side and pull off our running shoes, then strip off our T-shirts. I study the lake. It looks strange. Uninviting. I've never seen it like this.

Cody runs his fingers over my back. "Your tattoo's starting to heal. It looks good."

"Thanks," I say. A peace offering, maybe?

He pulls my hair back and kisses my neck.

I stiffen. "It's too hot, Cody."

He sighs and shifts away. "Have I been putting pressure on you?"

"No."

"So, what's wrong?"

"Nothing. I've just got a lot on my mind and I'm tired. You have no clue how much work it is looking after Jane...."

"Right," he sighs. "We can never stop worrying about Jane."

"What's that supposed to mean?"

"It means that maybe Jane needs to learn that everything isn't about her."

"You're jealous of Jane?" I ask. "Seriously?"

"No. But our relationship is important, too. And it doesn't seem like it is to you. Do you care about anything that's important to me? Clearly not the rodeo."

I knew it. He's been waiting to bring that up. I told Cody once that he can be very childish. He told me I get mad way too fast. I feel suddenly furious now, and hot.

I stand up. "I'm going swimming."

I step over the sizzling stones.

"Come back here," he says.

I wade into the lake, stepping carefully around rocks, mud oozing up between my toes. The water's tepid, not at all refreshing, but I start to swim. Breaststroke to keep my face out. It's like a dirty bathtub in here.

Then he's behind me, pulling my feet. I shriek, suck in a mouthful of water, spit it out. It tastes awful. We swim back to the shore together, standing up at the water's edge, waist deep. We stare at each other. We're covered in tiny black things. Our stomachs, hands, arms, shoulders, the dripping ends of my long hair. We've been swimming in a sea of burnt pine needles.

We burst out laughing. Then he kisses me, and I kiss him back because he looks so funny with burnt pine needles stuck all over him.

This is what it's like with Cody and me.

# CHAPTER THIRTY

"Jane!" I holler. "Get in here right now!"

"I'm busy."

"Now!"

Jane appears in my bedroom door. I hold out the empty ring box. "Where is my ring?"

"You didn't want it anyway."

"Where is my ring?"

She bursts into tears.

"I'm waiting," I say.

She sniffs. "I took it outside. To show Lucy and Bella. When you were swimming."

"Were you wearing it?"

"Yes. And then it was just gone."

A new wave of tears.

There's a loud roaring in my ears. I fight back the urge to panic. "Where were you when you last noticed it?"

"I don't know," says Jane.

Shit. How much did Cody pay for it? Maybe it *was* a real emerald. I never asked, and he never said. I can't tell him I lost it. I just can't. Then I get a crazy idea. There's only one place he could have bought it. Sanderson's Fine Jewelry on Birch Avenue in Hundred Mile. I'll go in and buy a replacement. Use my money from Wagonroad's.

It's a stupid idea.

*Breathe.*

I can't breathe.

What am I going to do? How can I give him the ring back when I don't have it?

"Think, Jane," I say. "What were you doing outside?"

"Picking daisies," she says. "In the hayfield."

~

Jane's grounded.

"You are absolutely forbidden to step one foot in my room," I say. "I will flush you down the toilet if I find you in here. Is that perfectly clear?"

She puts her hands on her hips. "Until when?"

"Christmas."

~

Jane takes her blood pressure.

"You're still grounded," I say.

~

Martin comes over while I'm washing pots. I watch Wayne through the kitchen window. He hobbles over to Martin's truck, and Martin takes something long and thin out of the back and hands it to Wayne. It looks like some kind of ski pole. Then he drives away.

# CHAPTER THIRTY-ONE

"Jane, go find Papa and tell him I've made some lemonade," I say.

She's back in a flash. "He's in the hayfield."

"What do you mean 'he's in the hayfield?'"

"I can see his cowboy hat moving around," she says.

Has Wayne gone completely crazy? I put the jug of lemonade in the fridge and grab my water bottle.

He's trudging slowly through the long grass, stooped right over, sweeping the pole back and forth. There's a strap around his wrist, some kind of control screen partway down the pole, and a big round disc at the bottom. When Jane and I catch up to him, I say, "What is that thing and what are you doing with it?"

*Beep, beep, beep.*

He ignores us and makes two more circles in the grass.

*Beep, beep.* Louder now.

"Ha!" Wayne bends down and picks up a piece of rusty metal.

It's evening, but the sun still feels like it's beating down on us. There's not a breath of anything moving in the grass. Sweat's pooling in the small of my back.

"It's a metal detector," he says. "I'm looking for a ring."

Jane bursts out, "I'm sorry! I wasn't supposed to tell but you were so mad!"

God. Who invented little sisters? But I'm distracted by Wayne. He doesn't look good. He's on the verge of heatstroke or another heart attack or something. He sips from my water bottle then says, "I'm okay now."

"No, you're not. Go back to the house, get some lemonade from the fridge, and sit in front of your fan," I say. "We'll keep looking."

He heads off without a fight and that freaks me out even more.

Jane and I wander around the field, waving the magic wand, searching in all the clumps of daisies. I can tell that Jane adores the metal detector though she's pretending she doesn't. She knows it's her fault we're tromping around this boiling hot field. We find a pocketknife, a twisted horseshoe, some fat nails, and a bunch of weird-shaped metal pieces.

I send Jane back to the house for a bucket because I don't want the horses stepping on this junk and getting hurt. As she wades through the grass toward me, bucket swinging, she shouts, "Have you found it yet?"

*Beep, beep, beep.*

I bend down, hopeful.

A metal disk, orange with rust. I drop it into the bucket.

~

Wayne picks up each chunk of metal in our bucket with his weathered work hands and identifies it. A clevis pin, the tooth of a diamond harrow, the guard from the mower, a shackle, a hitch pin. A rancher's vocabulary.

The rusty relics of Wayne's life.

~

Jane found her smelly felt pens under her bunk bed. Tonight's happy face is chocolate.

"Four sleeps till Nana comes home."

~

"Rachel, am I still grounded?"

"No."

"Can I come in your room?"

"Yes."

She leaps onto the bed beside me. She's had a bath, and I washed her hair, her pajamas are clean, and she knows where her show-and-tell is for tomorrow.

She cuddles into me. She smells like pineapple shampoo.

~

1 A.M.

Cody and I never resolved our fight. We just dodged it. I'm thinking about this when I get his text.

Cody: You still awake?

Me: Sort of

Cody: Sorry

Me: I'm sorry too

The stuff he said about Jane? I'm not going to change how I am with her. And I'm not sorry about that. When she burned her arm, that was the one time I didn't keep her safe. I'm not going to let that happen ever again.

But I am really sorry about the tattoo. I should have told him and let him go with me. I hurt his feelings, and I didn't mean to. I should have told Carlee, too. So why didn't I? Is this what Amber meant by me holding myself back?

When we fight, it's always Cody who says sorry first. Next time, it'll be me.

~

6 A.M.
Too hot to sleep. Wayne's up, too. We have coffee together and listen to the early weather report.

~

*Predicted high today: 97.0 degrees*
*Chance of precipitation: 0 percent*

# CHAPTER THIRTY-TWO

Jane scratches all through breakfast, her hand snaking inside her T-shirt.

"What are you doing?" asks Wayne.

"I'm itchy."

Wayne puts down his piece of toast and heaves himself off his chair. He leans over Jane and pulls up the front of her T-shirt. She's covered in red welts.

"What the hell's this?" he says.

Jane bursts into tears.

"Measles?" I start listing every highly contagious disease I know. "Scarlet fever? Chicken pox?"

"Fleas," says Wayne.

"Jane has fleas?"

Jane howls even louder.

"Mr. Boney has fleas," says Wayne. "That's it. That damn cat is moving out."

"Where to?" sobs Jane.

"The barn."

~

"Mr. Boney will have a job," says Wayne. "Animals love having jobs."

"What job?" asks Jane. She's lying on an old towel on the purple couch in the living room with just her underpants on. Her legs are covered with red bumps, too.

"Catching mice," says Wayne.

Jane sighs. "I guess he might like to do that." She starts scratching again.

"Stop that or you'll get scars," says Wayne.

He spreads bright pink calamine lotion on her tummy. He moves to the burn on her right arm where the puckered skin is now sprinkled with red welts.

"Aren't you girls supposed to be going to school today?" he says.

"Rachel says it doesn't matter in June," says Jane.

I can't kick either of her legs because they're on the couch.

"And anyway, we voted again," she adds. "We voted no. And it's Monday. Me and Rachel like staying home on Mondays."

"When I was a student, there were truant officers catching kids like you," says Wayne. "Now if you girls could give me some peace, I've got a book to write."

"I've got to feed the dogs," I say. "You stay here, Jane, until the ointment dries."

When I come back, everything is bright pink. The towel, her underpants. A bit of the couch.

And Jane.

~

I duct tape a piece of cardboard over the window in Mr. Boney's house. I put on the oven mitts, pounce and scoop, and drop him, hissing, into the box. I slam the flaps down and duct tape them shut.

"He needs an airhole," says Jane.

I carefully cut a slit with a kitchen knife.

"The barn is full of mice," says Wayne. "Mr. Boney has one week to learn how to hunt. After that, he's cut off. No more cat food."

Jane and I head outside. Jane brings Mr. Boney's water bowl, a ziplock bag of kibble, and an open can of tuna. Mr. Boney smashes against the side of the box that's pressing against my stomach. I can just barely hold on. The slit is tearing, and I see orange fur.

"He's breaking out!" yells Jane.

I drop the box on the cement floor, right inside the barn door. "Look out!"

The box heaves up and down like a ship on the ocean. I tear off the duct tape and leap back. The box crashes over. Mr. Boney blasts out, his paws splayed, his orange fur standing straight up.

Jane holds out the can of tuna. "Tuna! Yum yum!"

He streaks out the open barn.

"Hey, where are you going?" she shouts.

She drops the can of tuna and races after him. I get there just in time to see Mr. Boney dive under the log fence and vanish into the hayfield. The grass is a still, green sea. Not even a ripple.

"Shit," says Jane.

~

"Why can you say 'shit' and I can't?" says Jane.

"Because I make all the rules."

We're wading through tall, scratchy grass.

"Mr. Boney! Mr. Boney!" she calls.

It is ridiculously hot to be looking for a cat in a hayfield.

Finally, I say, "That's it. Mr. Boney will come home when he's hungry."

"Can you fix his house?" says Jane. "For when he comes back?"

"After I've done all the million other things I have to do," I say. "Cook food, water the garden, wash clothes, vacuum the house, clean up the—"

"He is coming back, right?" she says.

# CHAPTER THIRTY-THREE

An email just popped up on my laptop screen. Subject line: PARIS EXCHANGE.

Three attachments.

Bonjour Rachel,

We're very pleased that you have expressed an interest in studying in Paris. We've attached two PDFs, a general application form and an application for financial assistance, and a printable brochure. Please note that we will also need a transcript of your high school marks for the past two years.

If you have any questions, don't hesitate to ask. We hope to welcome you into our program.

À bientôt,

Amélie Dumont

Directrice des admissions

I print all the pages. I'm going to have to make my application perfect. Can I really do this? Me?

~

I'm going to burst. I have to tell someone. Carlee's my first choice. I call her from my bedroom.

"Wow," says Carlee. "Paris. That's your dream, Rach. Do Wayne and Margaret know you're applying?"

"Not yet. And I'm already stuck on the application. There are so many freaking questions. I need your help."

"Fire away."

"Okay," I say. "'How well do you cope with challenges?'"

"What's your biggest challenge?" she asks. "Don't even think about it. Just say."

"Jane."

"Keep going."

"I grounded her for losing my ring and told her I'd flush her down the toilet. I could be looking way harder for Mr. Boney, but I'm not. And all she's really done is miss Margaret."

"Good point. Your other biggest challenge?"

"Wayne. But let's not even go there."

"Okay," says Carlee. "I'll give you a B+. For effort."

"I just thought of something else," I say. "I put egg sandwiches in Jane's lunch kit two days in a row."

"She hates egg sandwiches," says Carlee. "You're demoted to a C. When are you going to tell Wayne and Margaret?"

"When Margaret gets back."

"But Cody knows?"

"No."

"Rachel. That's not fair to Cody."

"But he won't like it," I say.

~

She's right. I'm not being fair. You'd think I'd know that after my tattoo.

Cody's phone rings and rings. He's probably in the round pen working with Acorn. Why do I feel relieved? I haven't done anything wrong. I'm just about to disconnect when he picks up.

"Rach?"

I don't say anything.

"Rachel?"

I'm a moron. He can see it's me. "Hi," I say.

"Look, I'm trying to work with Acorn right now and it's not going great." He sounds exhausted. "Can we talk later?"

He's obviously frustrated. But for some dumb reason I plunge ahead.

"I've got something to tell you."

He sighs. "Is this bad?"

"No. I'm going to apply for an exchange program in Paris." There. I said it.

Dead silence. A horse whinnies in the distance. Then he says, "What?"

"I don't even know for sure if I'll be accepted. It's...well, I think it sounds really cool."

"You don't mean this summer?"

"No. I mean next year. But just one semester."

"How can you go to high school in Paris?" he says. "You don't speak French."

"I know. It's an English-speaking school. But my French is getting better, and maybe I'd get fluent. I'd be staying with a French family."

I'm talking too fast, but I really want him to understand what this means to me. "Let me explain—"

"What's to explain? You've applied."

"I haven't applied. I probably won't even be accepted."

"Yes, you will. I said I'd talk about it later. I'm getting nowhere with Acorn and this whole quarter horse idea is starting to suck and I don't need—"

"But you're amazing with horses—"

"Let me finish talking, for once." What does he mean, for once? Then he says, "I've been thinking about lots of stuff. About us."

This time, I keep my mouth shut. My heart's racing. About us? What is he going to say?

"You don't want to wear the ring. I get it. But then you get a tattoo and keep it a secret. Now you're going to Paris and how long have you been planning that behind my back? I'm sick of this. What's fucking next, Rachel?"

I feel like I've been slapped. Cody never talks to me like that. "Nothing's next."

"So what semester are you talking about? The last one? In case you forgot, it happens to be my grad year. So, I get to go to all the parties by myself? That sounds like fun."

"I'm applying for the winter semester, January to March."

I should never have started this. I don't dare tell him that it depends on when there's a space available. That I might not have a choice.

"Well, that's nice of you."

My eyes sting. "I could bring the brochure and application form over and show them to you."

"Don't bother," he says.

He's gone.

He hates the idea. I knew he would. But it's more than that. This is totally new territory for us. It's the worst fight we've ever had.

~

Three sleeps till Margaret comes home. Wayne and I are counting, too.

# CHAPTER THIRTY-FOUR

*Predicted high today: 100.5 degrees*
*Chance of precipitation: 0 percent*

~

The last day of high school. Jane has one more week. We're mostly cleaning out lockers, signing yearbooks, and saying goodbye to teachers. After we pick up report cards, we're free to go. Everyone's going to the Seven Eleven to get slushies. I can't face Cody right now. I can't face anyone. I slip off by myself. It's dead quiet in town. I pass the community hall where a banner saying *Welcome Slack Lake* is sagging over the door. Three little kids are squirting each other with water guns on the sidewalk in front. What else is there to do when you're evacuated from your homes?

I think about the past school year. I survived. Is that all I can say about it? I had a few great teachers, I learned some interesting stuff, I had fun. But I also messed up. Now, I'd just like to get home. But the bus won't be here for a couple of hours. I've got time to see Harjit.

~

I show Harjit my application.

"The questions seem obvious at first, but then they're not obvious," I say. "I don't know what they're looking for."

"Let's do, 'What do you hope to achieve as an exchange student?'" she says.

"Um, I want to learn to speak French and immerse myself in the culture and meet new people," I say.

She wrinkles her nose. "That's probably all true, but it's predictable. Why do you really want to go to Paris?"

I tell her about the famous writers who hung out in cafés with other starving writers. How I'd like to wander around on the streets where they wandered and see what it feels like.

And I tell her about *Emily in Paris*.

"That's what you should say," she says.

~

Strawberry is the flavor of the day. You can smell Jane's calendar from right across the kitchen.

We're down to two sleeps. I vacuum every room in the house.

~

6 A.M.

Sometime in the night, the Slack Lake fire jumped across the Thompson River. It's all over the radio and the TV. The wind changed direction. Our fire of note is now a fire of concern.

One news guy calls it an escaped fire, which is just plain terrifying.

We're glued to the Hundred Mile radio station. The local elementary schools are closing now instead of next week. Jane forgets that this fire is bad news and yelps with joy.

~

7 A.M.

All of Aspen Lake is under an Evacuation Alert.

# CHAPTER THIRTY-FIVE

*Predicted high today: 101.0 degrees*
*Chance of precipitation: 0 percent*

~

Jesse calls. There's a community meeting at the hall tomorrow at three o'clock. He'll come to our place first with his horse trailer to pick up our horses.

Margaret calls. I put her on speakerphone. She just talked to Susan who's afraid to drive down to the ferry to pick her up. "I'm still coming home tomorrow," she says. "I'll take the bus."

"I don't want you on the highways," says Wayne. "There are fires burning everywhere."

They argue, and Margaret wins because she's determined to get home. Then Uncle Rob calls, all the way from Poland. The fires in BC are headline news everywhere.

Uncle Rob sends a link to a site and waits on the phone until I have it up on my laptop. We look at it together.

**EVACUATION ALERT**

1. Prepare to leave your home on short notice.
2. Have your emergency kit and important documents ready to go.
3. Prepare your Grab and Go bags, which should include several days' clothing, medicine and prescriptions, and comfort items for children like a favorite toy to keep them busy.
4. Pack leashes, food, and carriers for pets.
5. Connect garden hoses and fill large containers with water to assist firefighters and help slow advancing flames.
6. Consider collecting precious photos and mementos that cannot be replaced.

"Can you do all that, Rach?" Uncle Rob says.

"Yes. I'm just not sure about the documents."

"Passports, house insurance, bank stuff. All that stuff's in Dad's room, in that filing cabinet by his cupboard. I went through it last time I was home. Take everything and put it in a big box."

Uncle Rob's on it. If only he were here.

"Okay," I say.

"There's an emergency first aid kit in the barn."

"Got it." My mind's spinning in overdrive, making lists.

"Good girl," he says. "And one more thing. Don't listen to Wayne."

~

Jane adores her Grab and Go bag.

So far:

Five Nate the Great books

Crayons

Coloring books

A marble game

Play-Doh

Stuffed rabbit

Stuffed penguin

A bag of cookies

"Whoa!" I say. "We're not moving out."

"What if we're gone for a year?" says Jane.

"Try thinking one week. Ask yourself, what would I absolutely need for a week? Like pajamas. Two clean T-shirts. Underpants. A toothbrush. And," I add sternly, "everything's gotta fit in your duffel bag."

"How am I supposed to take my bones?"

"You can't. Well, maybe two small ones."

"Three."

A leg, a rib, and a piece of a hip join the pile.

At the last minute, Jane grabs the bow and arrows that Wayne gave her for her seventh birthday. We squeeze them in along one side of the duffel bag.

She holds the two edges of the bag together while I struggle with the zipper.

"Wait!" she says. "I forgot my cow skull! I don't need pajamas or—"

I refuse to look at the empty eye sockets staring at me from above her door. I coax the zipper the last inch.

"The cow stays home."

My Grab and Go bag:

My *ruff night* nightshirt with dogs on it

Spare toothbrush, toothpaste, hairbrush, makeup, and cleansing pads

Sunscreen

Three tank tops

Both my bikinis

Two bras and some underpants

A pair of jeans

A pair of shorts

A photo in a black frame of me and Cody in the snow

Most of my photos are on my phone, but this one I printed and put on my dresser. I pause in my packing and sit on my bed with the photo. We're wearing parkas and we'd just got back from snowshoeing. It was my first time on snowshoes and the snow was so deep and I kept falling over. Cody was killing himself laughing, and that made me laugh too, and it was just so much fun.

I wrap the photo in a T-shirt and put it in my duffel bag. I leave enough room for my laptop, Kindle, and blow-dryer. They can go in last minute. This is what I can't take:

The lake

The loons

The old house

The marsh

My canoe

Mom's Butterfly House

Magic

~

"Grab and Go bag?" says Wayne. "Why the hell would I want to do that?"

"At least pack up your research papers," I say. "And all your photographs, your notes, all the stuff for your new book. You can't risk losing everything you've been working on. That would be stupid."

I gaze around his room. "I'll do it with you. I'll get some boxes so we can keep everything organized."

"You listen to me, girlie...," says Wayne.

Not now.

~

What would Margaret put in her Grab and Go bag?

Her garden.

# CHAPTER THIRTY-SIX

The three major highways into the interior of BC close.

Margaret can't get home.

Jane erupts into tears and runs outside, slamming the mudroom door.

# CHAPTER THIRTY-SEVEN

Jane's curled up beside Wayne on the purple couch. Bella's couch. She's there, too, sprawled at one end, snoring. Lucy's chewing her rubber ball on the carpet.

"Me and Papa are talking about the olden days," she says. There are traces of dried tears on her flushed cheeks.

I flop down beside Lucy. "That sounds interesting."

She launches into a long story. She's found out that when Wayne was a kid, he used to ski right through the old house. He made a path of snow on the wooden boards. Then—*whoosh!*—in the back door, through the room with the old stove, and out the front door.

"It's true," Jane finishes. "Right, Papa?"

"You bet it is."

It's...possible. The old house is at the bottom of a long, sloping field. Perfect for take-off. And the thing is, I can picture it. Snow piled up on the roof. The marsh buried in a blanket of white. Only the tops of wooden fence posts sticking out. A miniature Wayne, cheeks red from the cold, swooping through the house on skis. Old-fashioned wooden skis. Great-grandmother Mary flapping her apron. She's not really mad. Who could be mad at a boy skiing through your house?

Layers of history.

"I could do with some snow right now," I say. "Nice, freezing-cold, icy snow melting down my back. That would feel divine."

"I'm going to try it in our house," says Jane. "When it snows. Right, Papa?"

"Why not?" says Wayne.

"Our house isn't built on a hill," I point out. "You need a hill."

Jane looks at Wayne. "I'll figure out something," he says.

He will. He'll be out there, mounding up snow with his tractor. Screw the arthritis. He'll build a mountain for Jane. He'll build her a whole mountain range. Just so she can ski through our house. He'll build her Mount Everest.

~

I'm boiling a big pot of water for spaghetti. I've raised the temperature of the kitchen by at least ten degrees. Sweat's trickling down my neck. I search the pantry cupboard for spaghetti noodles. All I can find is an unopened package of whole wheat penne.

It takes forever to cook. Margaret's spaghetti sauce erupts in the microwave, splattering the inside with red blobs. When I finally have everything ready, I carry a tray with our plates and forks outside to the verandah and put it on a round table. Wayne's reading. "At last," he hmphs.

I glance around for Jane. A skinny, bare, brown leg is dangling over the edge of the hammock. Bella and Lucy are sprawled out underneath in the shade. "Dinner's ready!" I shout.

The leg disappears. Jane's head pops up. "About time!" she yells back.

I go to the kitchen for glasses of water. When I get back, Jane's on the verandah, staring at her plate.

"I thought you said we were having spaghetti," she says.

"It's penne. Same thing."

"No, it's not."

"It's pasta, Jane. It doesn't make any difference."

"I wanted spaghetti."

"It tastes exactly the same."

Her face darkens. "No."

"Yes."

"And I just wanted butter. I *detest* sauce."

"It's Nana's sauce."

She picks up her plate and a fork. "Fine. I'm going to the hammock."

"You'll make a mess—"

"Let her be," says Wayne. "She's having a hard day."

I collapse in Margaret's chair and take a long gulp of water, my eye on Jane. When she reaches the hammock, she looks back, then turns her plate upside down, flipping the penne and sauce onto the grass. Both dogs lunge for it.

I leap up. "You little brat!"

I have never called Jane a brat before. We glare at each other across the lawn.

"It's your fault Nana went away!" she screams.

"Don't think you'll be getting anything else to eat tonight," I yell back. "I got better things to do than cook for you!"

"I hate you!"

She races toward the side of the house. No way I'm chasing her. "Did you hear me?" I holler after her. "Nothing! You're going to bed hungry!"

She's vanished. I walk over and pick up her plate and fork. The penne's vanished, too, and the dogs are licking the grass in a frenzy. They grin up at me, their faces red with sauce.

Wayne hardly touches his dinner.

"Margaret always makes a salad when we have spaghetti," he says.

"Where have you been? It's not spaghetti, it's penne! That's the whole problem. And Margaret, in case you didn't notice, is not here." I pick up my fork and then slam it down. "And don't you dare give Jane any food tonight. She doesn't get a thing to eat until morning. She has to learn her lesson. Agreed?"

Wayne nods.

My eyes swim with tears. I chew a piece of penne. It's undercooked and the sauce is tepid.

"Why would anyone cook spaghetti on such a hot night?" says Wayne.

~

1 A.M.
I creep past Jane's closed door so I won't wake her. It's too hot to sleep and my stomach's growling.

I hear voices in the kitchen before I get there. Wayne and Jane. Coconspirators. They're at the table, hunched over big bowls of Rice Krispies. They look so guilty that I burst out laughing.

"Make room for me," I say.

~

I'm sleeping in Jane's room. Me in the top bunk, her in the bottom. Until this whole nightmare's over and we can go back to normal.

Until it rains so hard that it puts the fire out.

Until Margaret comes home.

# CHAPTER THIRTY-EIGHT

7 A.M.
*Predicted high today: 103.0 degrees*
*Chance of precipitation: 0 percent*

~

"What's this for?" says Jane.

She holds up a small, clear, plastic box. We're in the storage shed. While I hunt for some of Wayne's old cattle ranching magazines, Jane's digging through a carton of junk. It's something to do.

The plastic box is dusty and green in the corners but not cracked.

"No clue," I say.

We go back to the house and find Wayne in his bedroom, writing. "Delivery." I drop a stack of magazines on his desk.

"What's this, Papa?" asks Jane.

"It's for water bugs," says Wayne. "The lid is a magnifying glass. You put water in the box and you catch a water bug. Then you can study it. Your mother loved this."

Mom used this little box to look at bugs? My stomach does a little flip. It always does when we find something that was Mom's.

"There should be a net somewhere," says Wayne.

"I know where it is!" Jane races off. She's back at warp speed with a small green net, like they use for scooping up goldfish in an aquarium in a pet store.

"Every living creature you take out of the marsh goes back, Jane," says Wayne.

He's very eco-minded. I'm with him on this.

~

I sit in the grass on a small bank beside the marsh while Jane sloshes around, the net in one hand and the box in the other. She's Dr. Livingstone, I presume, except she's wearing pink shorts. I've sprayed all her bare skin with mosquito repellant, but there are no mosquitoes today. It's like that some days. Too hot even for mosquitoes. I've put her hair up in a messy bun and there are red lumps on the back of her neck from blackflies.

She wades in and out of the murky water, carrying her prisoners. We take turns examining them through the magnifying glass.

I can identify a water strider, that's all. I'm not into bugs. But it's mildly interesting looking at them. My favorite is a round little guy who looks like he's rowing a boat and keeps crashing into the sides of the box. My least favorite has big, bulging eyes, lots of legs, and three pointy tails.

In between specimens, I watch two mallards drifting in lazy circles in the reeds. When the sun hits their heads just right, they shimmer with turquoise, emerald-green, purple. Dragonflies are clicking their wings. The sun's warm but not baking hot yet. The temperature will start soaring after lunch.

Jane abandons bugs and tries to catch minnows instead. The ducks disappear and the dragonflies are suddenly quiet. Even the old house is sleeping.

Then there's a long, mournful meow.

"Mr. Boney!" Jane sploshes to shore and flings her net in the grass. "Rachel, look! He's on the old house!"

I turn around. Mr. Boney's crouching on the highest point of the roof, a lump of orange fur against the blue sky.

"What are you doing up there?" yells Jane.

Mr. Boney swishes his tail, lets out another cranky meow, and disappears through a dark hole in the mossy shingles.

~

We search the house. It doesn't take long. First, the big, bare room downstairs. Not very many hiding places there. Jane peers behind the old woodstove, and I look in the cupboard with the door half swinging off its rusty hinges.

"Mr. Boney, where are you?" shouts Jane.

We check out the two little rooms upstairs, the empty one where dry leaves have blown in through an open window frame and our secret room. There are tufts of orange fur on the old sleeping bag.

"Aha!" I say. "A clue."

"This is where he sleeps," says Jane. "This is his house now. So where is he?"

"He's gone hunting for his lunch. Cody and Jesse will be here soon and we gotta get back. Let's go."

When we step outside into the sunshine, it feels different. Duller. The sky has turned hazy, like it's covered with a veil. I look over the marsh, in the direction of Little Fort and the Slack Lake fire, and the sky is the same there. It's a flat white disc hanging over us. It makes me feel uneasy.

Instead of walking up the old tractor road, we climb through the field. It's hotter but shorter. Jane drags her feet. "There's too many thistles in here. And why do we have to go back now? I want to find Mr. Boney. Please, please, please."

"Stop that."

"Why are you so mad?"

"I'm not mad."

"What's that smell?'

"I think it's smoke." I take Jane's hand. "But you don't have to be scared. Smoke can travel hundreds of miles from a fire. Okay?"

"Okay," she says. "But it's freaky."

"Agreed."

Smelling smoke on a summer day is very freaky.

# CHAPTER THIRTY-NINE

Magic plants his front hooves on the ground, right at the edge of the metal ramp into Jesse's horse trailer. His tail swishes. The whites of his eyes flash.

Jesse has friends who have a big ranch near Meadow Lake, on the other side of Hundred Mile. He made two trips out there with their horses super early this morning and he's planning on taking ours tomorrow. He'll keep them at their place tonight. Dancer and Dixie scrambled into the trailer easily, plunging their noses into buckets of oats. Jesse, Cody, and I have been fighting with Magic for forty-five minutes. Jane's standing on the ledge on the side of the trailer, patting Dixie through a small, square opening. Wayne's watching from the kitchen window.

I'm holding Magic's lead rope, and Cody's standing behind him, slapping his butt with a long lunge whip. One hoof clatters onto the ramp, then another. I hold my breath. This is the closest he's got. "Come on, boy," I beg. "Come on!"

Magic rears up, yanking the rope from my hands. His hooves crash down on the metal, and he skitters off the side of the ramp. Dust churns up. I grab the rope, but I can barely hold on. He's prancing, snorting, his neck arched. His sides, slick with sweat, heave.

"Stay out of the way, Jane!" says Jesse. "Get up on the fence."

Jane jumps off the trailer and scrambles up on the log fence. I lead Magic in a tight circle. We try again.

"You gotta hit him harder than that, Cody," says Jesse.

Cody's face tightens. He and Jesse argue all the time about the best way to handle horses.

Magic braces his feet at the ramp, lowers his head, and blows air through his flared nostrils. Then he backs up fast, and I stumble and fall onto the ground. I get up, while Jesse grabs Magic's rope. "You okay?"

"Yeah." But my heart's racing.

"Jesus. For an old horse, he's got a lot of fight," he says. "He's wound himself right up. He's just not gonna go in."

Wayne joins us, leaning heavily on both canes.

"Let me try again," I plead.

I turn Magic in another circle. He whinnies, and Dancer calls back from inside the trailer.

Cody pulls off his black T-shirt and uses it to wipe the sweat off his face. "I think it's all the smoke. It's freaking him out."

The sky is dull, and the smell of smoke penetrates everything.

"It's not the smoke," says Wayne. "Magic was always a son of a bitch to load. We had a hell of a time getting him to the rodeos when Layla was barrel racing."

He's talking about Mom. She trained Magic to be a barrel racing horse. She'd hate this.

"I remember." Jesse glances at his watch.

I don't want Magic to be the only horse left here. I stroke his neck. "Come on. You gotta do this. Please."

Magic rears for a second time at the ramp and smashes down hard.

"He's got a stubborn mindset now," says Jesse. "I'll take Dancer and Dixie now they're loaded, and we'll try Magic again tomorrow. I probably won't be able to get out here until the afternoon. Then tomorrow night, I'll take all your horses out to Meadow Lake."

"Don't know why you're taking the horses, anyway," says Wayne. "Hell of a lot of work for nothing."

"We gotta go, Cody." Jesse sounds exhausted. "Rachel, an alternative is Magic stays and you leave him a trough of water and open all the gates so he has an escape route."

"Are you serious?" I feel sick.

Cody frowns. "What if we—"

"I can't spend any more time on this right now," says Jesse. "I got a list as long as my arm of stuff to do. Sorry, Rachel."

Cody slams the metal door at the back of the trailer shut, harder than he needs to, and slides down the latch.

"Put Magic in the corral behind the barn, Rachel," says Wayne.

"I'll go with you," says Cody.

"Five minutes," says Jesse.

When we get to the corral gate, I slip Magic's halter off, stroke his neck, then let him go. He paces up and down the fence, whinnying, stirring up dust.

"The fire's still down in the valley," says Cody. "This is just an alert. We got time. There's no way we'll have to evacuate anyway."

My throat closes.

"I'll see you later at the meeting." He puts his arms around me. "Hey. He'll be okay. We'll get him in tomorrow." I press my face against his chest. He's sweaty, but I don't care. Our fight over the Paris application was so stupid. All our fights are stupid.

The fire traveled nine miles before in one night. What if tomorrow's too late?

~

Carlee calls. Life is still normal in Rocky Lake.

"Hey," she says. "I'm sending moral support."

# CHAPTER FORTY

The parking lot in front of the community hall is packed with cars and trucks. I find a parking place for our truck, not far from Jesse's brown pickup. I leave the windows wide open so we won't cook when we get back in. I spot Martin's truck, too, and Amber's orange Rav4.

It's smoky. I can't tell where the sun is exactly, but I find it, a faint glow in a grayish haze. We walk toward a wooden outdoor stage with rows of the metal chairs from inside the hall set up in front. Some people have brought lawn chairs, others are perched on the tailgates of trucks. Kids and dogs are racing around.

Jane sees Cassie and Amber and races off. Martin stands up and waves. He's saved Wayne a chair in the front row. Wayne walks slowly, leaning heavily on his canes. I know each step is hurting him today, but he hides it. Wayne and Martin have ranched side by side for fifty years, birthing stubborn calves in the middle of the night, enduring winters of minus forty. Wayne thinks he has to look strong in front of his best friend.

The sign above the front door of the hall says *Daryl Bird Community Hall.* Wayne glances up at the name before he sits down heavily on his chair. Who gets to have a building named after their family?

On the stage, a woman in a gray skirt and white blouse is talking to a man in an RCMP uniform. Two guys are fiddling with a long cable that goes between a microphone on a stand. There are more people I know: Peggy from the store; three women who were at Mom and Uncle Jimmy's Celebration of Life; Edna, who drives the school bus; and Jane's teacher, Mrs. Layton.

I find Sarah and Emma and join them.

"Where's Cody?" says Sarah.

"He's coming."

A man in jeans and a black T-shirt taps the microphone a few times. Lee Finister, one of Jesse's friends. He runs the volunteer fire department here. "Okay," he says. "Let's get this started."

We listen quietly while Lee thanks the local First Nations for letting us have our meeting on unceded land. If you listened to Wayne, you'd think that the Birds were the first people here. But that's just not true. The Birds go back maybe two hundred years. But Carlee's family goes back thousands.

There are more people on the stage now. Lee introduces them. Lots of titles. The woman in the gray skirt is Janice Laird, our MLA. The Fire Chief from Hundred Mile is here, RCMP Sergeant Manny and two other police officers, a man and a woman with clipboards from the Ministry of Forests, a guy from the BC Wildfire Services, a woman from the Cariboo Regional District.

They read out a list of emergency phone numbers. Some people put them on their phones, others scribble them on pieces of paper. We've got the numbers beside our kitchen phone, so I stop listening.

Then there's a stream of reports. It goes on forever. The message seems to be *Don't panic. Not yet.*

Cody slips in beside me. I take his hand.

"You okay?" he says softly.

I nod. "Yeah."

I'm frying. I should have put more sunscreen on or worn one of Cody's baseball caps that he always leaves lying around our place. My head's throbbing.

We're into questions now. People shout them out and Lee repeats them into the microphone. Then someone on the stage comes forward and tries to give an answer.

It goes like this:

"Why wasn't the BC Wildfire Services website updated this morning?"

"We update every afternoon at—"

"How will we be informed if there's an order to evacuate?"

"You need to keep your radios and TVs on and keep—"

"Whose gonna see that we get compensation?"

"Whose gonna stop the looters?"

"All my officers will be working day and night to ensure that." Sergeant Manny wipes his forehead with his sleeve. "They already are—"

"Why doesn't the government—"

"Who decides—"

"One question at a time!" hollers Lee. "Be brief. If you all talk at once, no one can hear. And have some respect for the people up here. Everyone's working hard."

"What am I supposed to do with all my chickens if I have to evacuate?" a short, gray-haired woman yells.

People laugh, but I don't think she was trying to be funny. She turns to a woman beside her and waves her hands around. One of the police officers takes the mic and starts explaining the rules about livestock.

I glance out at the highway. It's oily black. Shimmering in the heat. There haven't been any cars for a long time. Everyone is here.

"We won't abandon you, Aspen Lake," says Janice Laird.

"We're going to wrap this up," says Lee. "We're all tired, and we need to get out of this heat. Remember, be safe. If you're asked to leave, go. We don't need any heroes to—"

Wayne stands up. "Not heroes," he says. "Just hard-working taxpayers who have a goddamn right to expect their property to be protected."

There's a hush. Wayne has the kind of voice that resonates without being loud. Everyone here knows his voice, and they're listening.

Someone calls out, "You tell 'em Wayne!"

"We've got livestock," says Wayne. "We've got homes we've built with our own hands. You're not making any progress getting this fire under control, but you're asking us to pack up and walk away."

There's a chorus of "Here! Here!" from the crowd.

"Do you have a specific question, sir?" says Lee. "If not—"

"Yeah, I have a question," says Wayne. "I know the kids have got to go, but is there a law that says I have to leave my property if there's an Evacuation Order?"

Janice Laird steps up to the mic again. "It's in everyone's best interests—"

"Is there a law?" says Wayne.

Janice Laird looks at Sergeant Manny. He takes the mic. "When people don't comply, they put all the emergency responders at risk. You have to trust—"

There's a rumble through the crowd. Someone at the front boos.

"Is there a law?" says Wayne.

The Fire Chief takes over. "If you don't comply with an Evacuation Order. . . ." He pauses, his eyes sweeping over the crowd. "If you refuse to leave, you need to fully understand that you'll be on your own. You can expect no services."

"We don't get them anyway," a man in a brown cowboy hat calls out, and people laugh.

"Even in an emergency," the Fire Chief continues, "like a life-threatening accident or a heart attack, an ambulance or a fire engine or any kind of first responder will not go onto your property. If telephone lines go down or the internet service is affected, you'll have no way of communicating. You won't be able to leave your property to get supplies or mail and expect to go back in. You won't have—"

"So, there is no law," says Wayne.

# CHAPTER FORTY-ONE

Someone's walking down our driveway toward the house. Slow, jerky steps. Weaving. I've just left the garden. I squint into the glaring sun.

Black cowboy hat. Two canes jerking like the stick legs of a gigantic bug. I meet him at the corner of the rail fence, just before he starts the downhill slope. "What are you doing?"

"What the hell do you think I'm doing?"

"Now? By yourself? The hottest part of the day? You always walk before bed." I glare at him. "How can you be so stupid? Do you want another heart attack?"

"You listen to me, girlie…you listen…."

He's done, not even enough gas left to insult me. His breathing is terrible; his knuckles, gripping the canes, are swollen into golf balls; his long, thin legs tremble in his faded jeans.

He's wearing his old brown plaid slippers.

~

I settle Wayne on his bed with his fan on full blast.

"You don't have to be mad at me," I say. "I rescued you. You should be mad at yourself. And don't pull that again. Ask me to go with you next time. And maybe we could go when it's not a hundred degrees outside."

He closes his eyes.

"I'll get you some water. And then I'm taking your blood pressure."

"I have excellent blood pressure," he says.

I go to the kitchen. Wayne's boots are on the floor in front of a chair near the door, where he always sits to put them on.

Abandoned, their long brown laces tangled into birds' nests.

~

Wayne's new numbers: 152 over 94.

*Worrying.*

~

4 A.M.

I'm staring at the ceiling above Jane's bunk bed, listening to Magic. He's been whinnying frantically since it first started getting light.

I slide my feet over the edge of the bunk, drop lightly to the floor.

Jane sits up. "Where are you going?"

"Outside. To see Magic."

"Me too."

We creep through the mudroom, trying not to wake up Wayne.

"What's the matter with Magic?" whispers Jane.

"He can't find Dancer and Dixie," I say. "He's lonely."

~

Jane and I come in the kitchen, wisps of hay sticking to our pajamas and smelling of horse. Wayne's in his plaid robe, drinking coffee. He has the radio on.

*Predicted high today: 104.0 degrees*

*Chance of precipitation: 0 percent*

We're breaking records.

~

7 A.M.

Jane's back in bed, asleep. I go out to the verandah, which at least is not like an oven. I've gone through my last stack of library books and I'm back on my Kindle. I've got a lineup of three books waiting, all by my favorite authors. I've brought out my application form, too.

I spread the pages on the table. Cody hasn't said a word about it. Not one word. I scan the questions and choose an easy one.

*How do I deal with loneliness?*

Easy. I read.

# CHAPTER FORTY-TWO

Every time I come into Margaret's garden, my heart sinks a little lower. Today, the garden's covered in a film of black specks. They're everywhere—on the paths, on the broccoli, the lettuce, the new beans, the raspberry canes, the beet tops, the blue Bachelor Buttons. The yellow daisies by the back fence are gray.

"What is it?" says Jane.

"Ashes."

"How did they get here?"

"The wind blew them," I say. "And don't walk in it. You're going to get filthy."

"The wind blew them from where?"

"I don't know. But ashes might be good for the plants. We'll wash them down into the soil."

We turn on the sprinkler and stand by the garden gate, watching the colors flood back into Margaret's garden—the blues, purples, greens, yellows. I give Jane a watering pail, and she sprinkles the daisies along the fence.

"Are these like Mom and Uncle Jimmy's ashes?" she says.

"No." I pick off a daisy petal and examine it closely. "I think these are more like cinders."

"What are cinders?" says Jane.

"I'm not sure, but they're different. See? This looks like a piece of a tiny, burnt pine needle."

Jane empties her watering pail on her bare feet. "I want to call Nana and tell her we washed her flowers."

~

Google:

*Ash: Gray, powdery material that remains after wood and similar materials have burned completely.*

*Cinder: A harder discreet piece of material that may have only been partially burned or may even still be burning.*

Does it matter?

It's what's left behind.

~

The old house is a mirage in the distance. It's shimmering. Or maybe I'm the one getting heatstroke. Beyond the house, the marsh is dull, mucky. There are brown weeds on the surface of the water, mud at the edges because the water level has dropped so much. A lifeless marsh.

This is the last time we're going to look for Mr. Boney. It's pointless to keep coming down here. It's too hot and Jane just gets upset and I'm sure Mr. Boney's dead.

Lucy and Bella have been looking halfheartedly for mice in the grass, too hot to make much of an effort. We beat our way through tall, brittle stalks to the doorway. A small doe leaps through the gaping window frame, making us jump. She often hides inside the house to escape the flies. She always surprises us. She springs through the dry grass like a kangaroo. The dogs look but don't chase her.

Jane climbs up the narrow staircase while I stay down below. "He's not here!" she shouts. "We should have brought some food!"

I gaze around. Dust motes dance in the sunlight slanting through the front window. There's a pile of deer poop in the corner.

Then Jane calls, "Come here!"

I climb the stairs to the little room where Mom played.

Jane's crouched beside the mattress. One end is torn apart and dirty. White stuffing is mounded up on top of the sleeping bag. "Something's been chewing this," she says. "I think it's Mr. Boney. He's making a bed."

"Maybe," I say.

"He needs water."

I get the old pot from downstairs, bring it up, and empty my water bottle in it. It's going to evaporate before Mr. Boney finds it. If he's even around still. Other animals drink at the marsh. Maybe he can, too.

"Where is he?" says Jane.

"That is the mystery." The air in here is thick. I can taste dust in my throat. This can't be healthy. "Let's go."

When we get back downstairs, I say, "Look up and listen."

Jane gapes at the rows of mud nests along the rafters. "What's making that noise?" she whispers.

"Baby sparrows."

# CHAPTER FORTY-THREE

There's a rumble outside, right over top of our house. It gets louder and louder, drowning Bella and Lucy's wild barking. Jane and I rush outside through the mudroom door.

A helicopter is hovering over our biggest horse corral, its huge propellers spinning. A giant pterodactyl. Dust swirls up in clouds, and the noise is deafening. Magic is in the next corral, galloping in circles, terrified.

"What's it doing?" yells Jane. She claps her hands over her ears.

The helicopter tilts from side to side, and then it almost seems to stop mid-air before it drops down, flattening the grass. It's going to land. *Here.* Life has gone completely insane. Who has a helicopter land in their front yard?

It plops onto the ground. Faces peer through the side window, and then a door opens. A man, crouching, shouts something. Maybe it's *Get back*. I grab Jane's arm, holding her while the propellors spin slower and slower and then, finally, stop.

Silence.

The man jumps down. He's in jeans and a black T-shirt. Another man, in dark pants and a short-sleeved blue shirt, climbs out after him, holding a clipboard. They walk toward the corral gate.

"Hello there!" the man with the clipboard calls out.

Crap. They're going to make us go with them. Now. Me, Jane, Wayne, the dogs. That's why they're here. We'll never all fit in the helicopter. And Magic? Who will look after Magic?

I hang onto Lucy and Bella's collars, ordering them to be quiet.

Behind us, Wayne's voice roars, "Get off my ranch!"

I spin around. Wayne's leaning on a cane, in his other hand is a rifle.

The men stop walking. "Are you Wayne Bird?" asks the man with the clipboard.

"I told you," says Wayne. "Get off my ranch."

The man takes a few steps forward. "We just want to talk to you about the fire. We want to ensure that—"

Wayne raises his rifle.

"Whoa, whoa, whoa." The man backs up.

"Let's all stay calm," says the other man. "Mr. Bird, please put the rifle down."

"Get off my ranch."

"Mr. Bird, I'm asking you to put the rifle down."

Wayne fires in the air.

~

The men run back to the helicopter and scramble inside. They leave in another blast of whirling blades and wind. We watch until it's a black speck in the hazy sky.

~

Three hours later, I'm watering Margaret's pots of petunias along the verandah when I hear the crunch of tires on gravel. Lucy and Bella start barking. I've been waiting for this. I turn off the hose and walk around to the front of the house. An RCMP car is parked beside the barn.

An RCMP officer and a different man with a clipboard are standing beside the car. The officer smiles. She says, "Hi there. I'm Leslie. And this is Jack Gilbert. He's with the Ministry of Forests."

"Hi," I say.

"We need to talk to Wayne," says Leslie.

I don't think this is negotiable. I take them inside.

~

We're all standing in the kitchen. Wayne doesn't ask them to sit down. He says, "Hello, Leslie. Make this quick. I've got work to do."

They know each other. Why am I surprised? Wayne knows everybody.

"We're checking on some of the more isolated properties," says Jack. "How are you folks doing?"

Wayne is stonily silent, so I say, "Fine."

"Just want to make sure you're aware that you're under an Evacuation Alert."

"Yes," I say. He really thinks we don't know?

"It's all precaution at this stage. Nothing to get stressed about. But we'll be checking in with your neighbors at High Valley Ranch as well. They're at the end of the road. You both have only one way out to the main highway. You don't want to get trapped in here."

"On a positive note, the news on the fire is quite promising this morning," says Leslie. "It's almost 50 percent contained now. We just want to keep everyone informed. Keep track of people."

I'm still fixated on what Jack said. Only one way out. We knew that, but hearing it out loud sends a chill down my back.

There's a form on his clipboard to fill out. He calls out the questions and I answer, and he writes it all down.

*How many people are currently living here?*

*Full names?*

*Ages?*

*Anyone with disabilities?*

He stares at Wayne's canes.

"You can walk on your own, sir?"

"Yes, he can," I say.

"Mr. Bird, are you the only adult currently living here?"

Jack and Leslie are keeping track of us. This is good. I should be more helpful. "My grandmother's away on Saltspring Island. She was supposed to be back, but now they've closed the highway."

"Right," says Leslie. "I'll leave you my card. And here's some information for you to read."

Printed blue paper, a business card stapled in the corner. I put it on the counter. "Thank you."

Jack checks his clipboard. Then he says briskly, "I'll need the name and phone number of your dentist."

Dentist?

Shit.

Our dentist's name is in Margaret's address book by the phone. Jack clears his throat and scribbles in his notebook. "Okay, that's all. We should get going. But before we leave, any questions?"

"When is your boss going to get off his ass and send in the army like he should've done two weeks ago?" says Wayne.

"Ha-ha. Actually, he's not really my boss." Jack clips all his papers together. "Right. You got good radio and TV reception here?"

Does he think this is Siberia? Then I remember that six months ago, before we got Wi-Fi, I thought this was Siberia. "Internet, too. We're checking in every day."

"Well, that's good to know. Keep yourselves informed. Stay safe, folks."

"I'm going to leave you my card," says Leslie. "Phone me if you have any questions or if you need any help. And one more thing. Section 87 of the Criminal Code, Wayne. We're all under a lot of stress, but threatening someone with a firearm without lawful excuse is an indictable offense. Up to five years in prison."

~

"Why did he want to know the name of our dentist?" asks Jane.

I never lie to Jane.

"They use dental records to identify burnt bodies," I say.

I dig around in the kitchen garbage where Wayne tossed the blue papers. I fish them out. Because you just never know.

Jane's dying to use her Grab and Go bag. "I wish we could evacuate." Then she looks at Wayne's face. "Just for two days."

# CHAPTER FORTY-FOUR

There's something I still need to do. I go into Margaret's room and shut the door behind me. It feels like trespassing, but I don't think she'd mind. It's suffocating in Wayne's room, but in here, there's a sense of peace. The wallpaper is so dated, huge bouquets of pink roses, but I love it. All her gardening books are in a green painted bookcase under the window. Beside her rocking chair is a big basket full of knitting yarn. Her glass birds are lined up on the windowsill.

I sit on her bed.

What would Margaret take?

Not just her garden.

Her family.

I remember the feeling the first time I went into Margaret's room and saw all these faces on her walls. It was like I'd stepped into a room full of people who had been there all along, waiting for me.

There are framed photos of Uncle Rob, Uncle Jimmy, and Mom on all the walls. Formal school photos for every grade. Casual photos taken all over the ranch. I wander around the room, stopping at all the photos of Mom. Red hair, pigtails, ponytails, short hair, braces. Every year getting prettier and prettier. Mom riding Magic, holding a blue rosette for barrel racing, blowing out birthday candles with Uncle Jimmy.

I've looked at all these photos so many times, but I never get tired of them. Each photo is framed with glass. I take them down carefully, almost reverently, one at a time, and lay them in a strong cardboard box. The last photo is the newest—me and Jane in the hammock. Two huge smiles.

More layers of history.

There are more things I could put in Margaret's Grab and Go bag, but I stop. I would hate someone to look through my stuff, decide what was important and what could be left behind.

I carry the box to the door. I look back at the bare wall before leaving.

I can't feel anything now.

Everyone's gone.

~

The air's smoky. Magic's nostrils flare. He's wet with sweat. He's been galloping in his corral, whinnying, since he heard the rumble of Jesse's truck and trailer. I lead him to the ramp, and I know he senses my anxiety. He stops. Braces his front legs. Whinnies again.

"Come on, boy," says Cody, tapping the whip on his butt. "You can do this."

Magic gives a huge shudder and scrambles up the ramp.

"He's in!" Jesse slams the door shut.

I feel incredible relief and sadness at the same time. How long will it be before we're all back here together? What if the worst happens and we have to evacuate and we never come back?

I lean through the open window on the side of the trailer and stroke Magic's neck. I try to absorb his smell. He's chomping on oats, but his ears swivel.

Cody comes up behind me and touches my shoulder, so I turn to face him. He's pulled off his baseball cap, and there's a dark line across his forehead. He looks wiped.

"Hey," he says. "I love the old guy, too, you know."

I nod. I should have realized that I'm not the only one who was stressed about Magic. That Cody would do anything to keep Magic safe. I'm afraid if I say something, I'll cry. So I give him a huge hug instead.

We stay like that, wrapped around each other. I don't think he wants to let go, either.

~

6 A.M.
*Predicted high today: 115.5 degrees*
*Chance of precipitation: 0 percent*

The heat dome is officially here.

I google it.

The best definition I find: *The lid on a pressure cooker.*

# CHAPTER FORTY-FIVE

Kwantan made the news tonight. It's the hottest place in Canada today. One hundred and twenty-one degrees. I've been to Kwantan with the volleyball team last fall. It took about three hours in the bus, and it's this little village, tucked into an arid canyon beside the Fraser River. A heat trap. There's not much there, but I liked it. The views of the canyon and the river are amazing. Everyone was super friendly.

People in Kwantan are stuffing wet blankets into windows to protect themselves from the heat. Apples are baking on the trees, cooking, and turning brown.

~

A gopher's floating in the old porcelain bathtub that we use for a water trough for the horses. Eyes glazed over. The sides of the tub are high. Did he smell the water? I imagine him scrambling up the fence behind the tub, creeping along the top rail, then tumbling in. How long did he swim in circles, trying to climb up the slippery walls, before he drowned?

I lift him out. His body is sodden and heavy. I carry him into the trees and lay him down in some tall grass. It feels like I should be doing something more, but I don't know what it is.

~

Kwantan burns to the ground. It's going viral around the world.

Wayne, Jane, and I are glued to the TV. "More than one thousand people were forced to flee a small village in BC's Fraser Canyon," says the anchorman on Global News. "They raced out of town as flames and smoke decimated their entire community."

More information keeps coming in. Ninety percent of the village is destroyed. Houses, the ambulance station, the stores, the RCMP detachment.

They play the same video over and over, shot from the front of a car as it cruises along the empty main street. You can't see much. Dense smoke and billowing orange flames. It looks surreal.

You can feel the mayor's emotion. "The whole town is on fire," he says. "It took only fifteen minutes from the first sign of smoke to, all of a sudden, fire sweeping through the village."

Then they talk to a woman who's crying. "Chimneys, charred cars, a cement wall. I've lived here fifty years. That's all that's left."

I think of the volleyball tournament and the kids from the Kwantan team. They were mostly First Nations. They won the trophy. What will they do now?

"Was that our fire?" says Jane.

"No," says Wayne. "A different one. How the hell did that happen?"

~

The temperature in the middle of the day has dropped by almost twenty degrees. Finally, relief from the heat. It's so sudden. A shock.

For Kwantan, it's too late.

# CHAPTER FORTY-SIX

"Rachel!" yells Jane. Her head is hanging out the upstairs window at the front of the old house. "Come here! Quick!"

I've long given up on Mr. Boney, but Jane hasn't. I've been sitting on a broken piece of fence, staring at the marsh, and contemplating life. More specifically, looking for ducks in the reeds. There's not much visible smoke today, but you can taste it. We survived the heat dome. I'm hoping that Magic, Dancer, and Dixie can come home soon. Margaret, too.

"Coming!" I yell back.

Jane's kneeling on the floor by the mattress. There's a big, messy clump of dirty gray stuffing in the middle of the sleeping bag. And a tangle of tiny bodies, curled together.

I kneel beside Jane. I can make out little ears, folded over, slits that could be eyes.

"What are they?" she says.

"Kittens, I think."

They're a mix of orange, gray, and black fur. I can't tell how many there are. They're all wrapped together.

"Where did they come from?" says Jane.

"They must be Mr. Boney's. There's no other cats anywhere near here."

I hear Jane draw in a quick breath. I put my hand out and gently touch a kitten. It's tiny body is rigid. I touch another.

"Oh no," I say.

"What?" Jane's starting to cry.

"They're dead."

~

I tug on the scrap of worn curtain at the window, and it rips loose from the nails. We lay the cloth on the floor, put some of the stuffing in the middle, and then lay the tiny kittens on top. Tears are flooding Jane's cheeks, dripping onto the kittens. We fold the curtain over them like a little package. Jane insists on carrying them.

She's so careful.

"They don't feel like anything," she whispers through her tears. "They're like feathers."

When we get downstairs, something doesn't seem right. I glance around. Bird shit, dirt, broken glass. Nothing's different. But it feels like it.

When we step outside into the sun, Jane says suddenly, "We can't leave Mr. Boney."

We walk through the long grass, calling him. "He's probably hiding down by the marsh," I say. "He'll be okay."

I don't really believe he's hanging out at the marsh. I'm sure he's dead, too.

"He'll think his babies have gone to heaven," says Jane.

"And now, we have to plan a funeral," I say.

~

Jane doesn't want kitten bones for her collection.

She just doesn't.

~

"There were five kittens," I tell Cody on the phone. "All dead. Mr. Boney is a female. We didn't know that."

"Jesus," he says. "How did Jane take it?"

"She's okay now. We're having the funeral in a few minutes. It was like a furnace in that little room. It's the only one that still has all its glass in the window. Wayne told me the kittens basically cooked. He thinks they've been dead for a few days."

"Shit, Rachel. Spare me the details."

"I'm just telling you. It was horrible."

"I get it."

Cody starts trying to figure out how he can get a ride over here tonight and then home again later. It's complicated. Finally, he abandons the idea.

I'm listening but I'm not. Through the living room window, I see Jane and Wayne walking toward the trees behind Margaret's garden. Wayne has a shovel, and Jane has a shoebox of dead kittens.

"I gotta go," I say.

I hang up, then close my eyes. Now I know what was different in the old house.

Silent nests.

~

Margaret calls. One billion marine animals on the coast died. They baked in their shells.

"The shore crunches when you walk on it because of all the empty mussel shells," she says. "It's already starting to reek here of decaying clams and sea stars. I need to get home, Wayne. I could fly to Kamloops and—"

"No," he says.

# CHAPTER FORTY-SEVEN

Wayne wants more sprinklers. The grass all around the house has dried up and turned brown. It's a huge fire hazard. He's going to start soaking it. Just in case.

The man who owns the hardware store in Hundred Mile knows Wayne. He says that everyone's looking for sprinklers, but there's a new shipment in, and he'll put two aside for us.

Amber takes Jane over to their place to play with Cassie and get her mind off the dead kittens. After lunch, Wayne and I drive into town. It's warmed up since this morning but nothing like before. We have the windows open and the breeze wafting in is almost refreshing. Wayne dozes off.

The sky is hazy, white. It's hard to tell if it's a cloud or smoke. It seems forever since it's been clear and bright blue.

Town is eerily deserted.

"Sorry," says the man at the hardware store. "There's been so many customers coming in. I can only give you one."

We pick up a garden hose, too, and then we cruise past Tim Hortons so Wayne can see if he recognizes any of the trucks in the parking lot. Shorty's blue pickup is here and Danny Mason's black pickup. Both old ranching buddies. I help him get inside and over to the corner table where his friends are drinking coffee and yakking. Three old men in cowboy hats, boots, and plaid shirts. It's just what Wayne needs.

I leave our truck and cross the highway to the bookstore. A sign on the door says *Closed.*

How am I going to kill an hour? It's Monday, so the library's closed, too. I'm making a vague plan of walking to Centennial Park when I hear someone calling my name. Carlee and her cousin Starla run across Birch Avenue, midway between the two crosswalks, and one of the few cars honks its horn.

"What are you doing here?" says Carlee.

"Buying a sprinkler. Wayne's having coffee at Timmy's. Hi, Starla."

"Hi," she says.

Starla's from Kwantan. I've met her lots of times. She's as athletic as Carlee. It's mainly because of her that the Kwantan team slaughtered us in volleyball.

"I'm really sorry about what happened," I say.

That sounds lame, it's not enough, but I'm not sure what else to say. I have no idea if Starla's house burned down. I don't know anything. I haven't talked to Carlee for days.

Starla kind of nods. It's obvious she's been crying. She always wears a lot of makeup, and her face is a puffy, streaky mess of mascara.

"We're going to A&W for food," says Carlee.

"I'll come, too," I say.

~

We find a booth at the back. I sit beside Carlee, Starla opposite us.

"Is my mascara running all over the place?" she asks.

"A teeny bit," says Carlee.

"Oh, God." Starla jumps up. "I'll be back in a minute."

She disappears to the bathroom.

"What's going on?" I say.

"Toby's dead."

Toby? Starla has four brothers. I can never remember all their names. I must look horrified because Carlee says quickly, "Starla's rescue dog. Remember? She got him last fall. She adored him."

"Right."

"He ran away during the fire. Someone found his body behind a trailer. They just heard. He burned to death."

"Shit. That's awful. I can't believe this is happening."

"They're all staying with us," says Carlee. "I was going to call you, but it's been crazy."

I think back to when she joked about having all of us come to her place if we had to evacuate. Carlee's house is not that big. "Where's everyone sleeping?" I say.

"Star's in with me, the boys are all on the floor in Jordie's room. Aunty Marnie and Aunty Sheila and Uncle Ray are at Grandma's house."

"Wow."

Carlee has a lot of family. They all look out for each other. She's lucky. My family was small to start with. Now Mom and Uncle Jimmy are gone. Sometimes I feel like I have to hold tight just to keep anyone else from disappearing.

"They lost everything, Rachel," says Carlee. "Everyone's houses burned to the ground. They got no warning. They had, like, ten minutes to get out. You should hear their stories. It was a nightmare."

"We watched on the news. It was unbelievable."

"Can you imagine losing everything you owned?"

"No, I can't."

"Aunty Marnie says she doesn't give a shit about the furniture and TV and stuff like that. She's kept these photo albums for years, the ones where you stick the pictures in, and they're all gone."

"That's so sad," I say.

"Everyone's mega stressed." Carlee gives a huge sigh. "Mom's snapping at Dad all the time and she's never like that. And I'm probably not going to get to do any barrel racing this year because the entry fees are so expensive, and Dad says we have a lot of extra people to feed and look after right now."

"But your points. You have to barrel race."

"It doesn't matter. It's not like there'll be a rodeo in Aspen Lake."

"It does matter," I say. "It doesn't mean that all the rodeos are going to be canceled just because Aspen Lake's is. Barrel racing goes right into the fall. You've been practicing so hard for the season."

"Yeah, well, I'm being a bitch to complain about barrel racing when Starla doesn't even have a home anymore...just a sec."

She takes her phone out of her bag, stares at her messages, frowns, and starts typing. For the first time, I feel completely shut out of her life.

She puts her phone away, glances past me, and says, "Starla's coming back. Don't say one word about me not barrel racing. She'll say it's all her family's fault. Come on. Let's go order."

~

I sip water and try not to smell the full power of their burgers and onion rings.

I'm not very good at consoling. I should be with all the practice I've had with Jane, but I'm not. I want to say something more to Starla, but what?

"Maybe you could rescue another dog that needs a good home," I volunteer.

As soon as it comes out, I know it's wrong. Really wrong.

Absolute silence. It's like everyone in A&W heard me and stopped mid-chew to gape at the insensitive moron.

"What I meant was…I didn't mean right…."

Starla bursts into sobs. Carlee shoots me the darkest glare possible. She jumps up and scoots over to the other side of the booth and hugs Starla. "I'm going to miss Toby so much, too," she says. "It's so fucking unfair."

Starla wipes her face with a serviette and sighs. "Thanks, Carlee."

"I'm really sorry," I say.

"Don't be," says Starla, a little cooly. "I'm okay."

You'd think I'd know by now. When something really crappy happens, forget positive thinking. Forget thinking you could replace your beloved dog with any other.

What really makes you feel better is when someone says, "It's so fucking unfair."

# CHAPTER FORTY-EIGHT

I'm in the hammock. Jane's with Wayne, so I don't have to worry about her. I'm listening to our new sprinkler go *tick-tick-tick* and watching the sky turn yellow. The sun has disappeared, and the light's getting stranger and stranger. The colors of the leaves on the trees and the roses along the fence are all wrong.

I tip out of the hammock and go back to the verandah. The colors are wrong here, too. The pink petunias, the butterflies in Mom's Butterfly House. Even the red of Wayne's plaid shirt isn't red anymore. It's a new, made-up color.

"You look really weird, Rachel," says Jane. "Do I look weird, too?"

"Super weird."

Jane and Wayne and I sit on the verandah and watch day turn into night. It's the eeriest thing. It takes less than fifteen minutes. I check the time of my phone. 3:05 pm. It's the middle of the afternoon, but it's also the middle of the night.

Lucy starts to whine. She's half under Wayne's chair. Bella raises her head and looks around. Lucy's whine turns into a high-pitched yowl.

"That's enough, Lucy," says Wayne.

Lucy gives one final yip, then she's quiet. It's completely still. Trees, the fence, you can't see anything. I'd need a flashlight just to walk to the hammock to get my Kindle.

My phone vibrates. A text from Amber:

Is it dark at your place?

A text from Cody: Crazy, huh?

I stare into the blackness. I can just make out the shapes of trees again. I put my phone down without answering.

We stay on the verandah, watching the night melt back into day.

~

3:50 P.M.

The sun is back. It's a normal sun. Whatever that means.

Cody calls. He's been online. "There was a famous day in the US when this happened, back in the fifties. At first, they thought it was UFOs. Then government experiments. Turned out it was a forest fire causing problems all the way from Canada. They called it Black Sunday."

Jane jumps down the steps onto the grass. Lucy chases her. Her bare feet and Lucy's white paws turn gray. It's ashes this time, not burnt pine needles. They're lying like a filmy blanket over everything. But it means the same thing.

This is our Black Monday.

~

4 A.M.
Wind.

I stand by my window, watching huge trees sway back and forth like they're made of rubber. Huge branches are being flung everywhere. A lawn chair is picked up, then slammed against the side of the verandah steps. There's a steady roar outside. My window rattles.

I go downstairs to the living room. Wayne hobbles out of his bedroom, and minutes later Jane's here.

We keep a vigil together.

Wind and fires are a fatal combination. You hear that all the time.

An enormous crash. Jane screams. Margaret's cherry tree that never has cherries, that she planted when she married Wayne, is down.

The lights blink. Once, twice, three times. The power's out. The room is gray with moonlight.

Jane wants candles and cookies.

~

5 A.M.
The wind has died to a moan. The lawn in the gray dawn light is littered with debris.

The phone rings.

It's Martin.

"Do you have the radio on?" he asks.

"No. Why?"

"The fire broke through its perimeter. Aspen Lake's under an Evacuation Order. Everyone's gotta go, Rachel."

# CHAPTER FORTY-NINE

5:30 A.M.

Martin calls back with a plan. "I'm taking Susan and Amber and Cassie to my sister's in Lone Butte. They can go on to Hundred Mile from there. We're going to leave right away. I've got my stock trailer hooked up. Shorty had four calves born last night. I'm going to pick them up on the way, get them out of there."

Shorty's cattle ranch is on the north side of Aspen Lake. "Last night?" I say. "Shit."

"Bad timing, for sure. Are you guys ready to go? You can follow us out."

I think of Jane, who finally collapsed into a deep sleep on the couch. Wayne, not one single thing packed. His bedroom's a cluttered museum of family papers, old books, black and white photos. "I need a bit of time. I can't rush Wayne."

"Alright. There's no big panic. The fire's still far away. But you gotta get out by eight. No later. We'll stop at your place on our way. Give you a hand."

I glance at my phone. Two and a half hours. "You don't need to. Jane can help me."

"Are you sure?"

"I'm sure," I say.

"You're okay driving the pickup?"

"Yes. Just go," I say. "The calves are important. We'll be fine."

"Okay. I'll drop off the calves, then head back to your place. Should be there by seven-thirty at the latest," he says. "I'll drive out behind you."

"We'll be ready."

Wayne's in his pajamas in his room, leaning against the windowsill, staring out. I carry in two big boxes and put them on the floor. "Pack up your papers. Everything for your book. All that work you've done. You can't lose it. That would be stupid."

His stony silence scares me. I want him to turn around, to say something, even "Girlie, what the hell are you doing?"

"We're going," I say. "As soon as Martin gets back, we're going. All of us. You've got to get dressed and be ready."

Jesse calls.

"Everything's good," I say. "Martin's coming back, and he'll follow us out.... Don't worry. We're safe."

Then Margaret. "The fire's still a long way away.... We're okay. We're safe."

"Let me talk to Wayne," she says.

~

On top of the ridge, a huge mushroom-shaped cloud of white smoke is rising into the dirty blue sky. It looks like an atomic bomb. It's something new that we haven't seen before.

In between loading the truck, Cody and I text back and forth.

We're heading out now, he says.

Me: Okay. Drive safe. See you in town

Cody: I love you

Me: I love you

All the evacuees have to go to the community center in Hundred Mile to register. They're also setting up cots for people to sleep and bringing in food. That's where we'll find each other.

Cody again: You guys should go.

Me: We're safe. We're going.

I slide my phone in the back pocket of my jeans. Everyone's left and we're still here. They've abandoned us. That's not fair, it's not even true, but it's how I feel. Abandoned and terrified.

~

6:30 A.M.

The Grab and Go bags, the box of documents and important papers, a sack of dog food, bottles of water, the photos from Margaret's bedroom, Wayne's medication, my laptop, charging cords, a box of food—it's all in the back of the truck.

Have I forgotten anything? Bella and Lucy are confined to the mudroom, so they can't disappear. Jane's been upstairs for an hour, basically emptying her room into Margaret's shopping bags. So much for Grab and Go. She's taking everything that's not attached to the wall or the floor.

I head into the garden to set up the sprinkler. I'll leave it on. Not that it will do any good. Almost everything looks dead. Flowers are drooping, the heads of broccoli are little yellow buttons, the bolted lettuce is limp. The soil around the new beans is hard and cracked. I did not do a good job looking after this garden. Margaret won't blame me, I know she won't, but I still feel terrible.

Something's caught in the green plastic netting that's draped over the strawberries. I crouch down to have a better look. A chipmunk, snagged by one tiny foot. His mouth is stretched open in a horrible grimace. There's a piece of half-chewed strawberry on the dirt under his tummy. Gently, I pry him loose from the net. I tuck his stiff, fried body into the long grass under the currant bushes.

Jane would like another funeral, and probably one for the drowned gopher, too. But there's not time. There's not enough time to say goodbye to anything. Not properly.

If I had time and Magic were here, I know where I'd go. I'd ride to the old house and the marsh. I'd ride to the top of the high hill where Jane found her first bone. I'd ride to Butterfly Lake. The lake that's not a lake anymore, the lake Mom named.

I'd find that old eagle, the King of Butterfly Lake. I'd ask him to save our ranch.

# CHAPTER FIFTY

6:45 A.M.

The kitchen phone rings. It's Uncle Rob. I give him a quick update.

*The fire's still a long way away...we're going...we're safe.* How do I even know that anymore? But I have to keep repeating it.

"Have you got lots of gas in the truck?"

"Yes. I filled it up at the store a couple of days ago. And Martin's coming back."

"Good. What's Dad doing? Is he cooperating?"

I have no idea if Wayne's cooperating. At least he's dressed now. I can see him through the kitchen window, struggling to set up a sprinkler in front of the house. Thick smoke has moved in now, and that's about as far as you can see. The corral fences and the barn are smudges, the atomic bomb above the ridge has disappeared into brown gloom.

"Let me talk to him," says Uncle Rob.

I take the phone outside. The air is acrid, stinging my eyes. "It's Uncle Rob," I say.

"Get the sprinkler from the garden," says Wayne. "And a hose. Margaret can always plant another garden. We've got to save the house." He reaches for the phone.

When I get back with the sprinkler and hose, the phone is laying on the grass. I pick it up and shove it in my pocket.

Wayne's staring at the house, breathing heavily. "There should be two more sprinklers in the garden shed," he says.

"It's not good for you to be breathing all this crap," I say.

"I want a sprinkler on each corner of the house. And we need more goddamn hoses."

~

7:15 A.M.

Martin calls from his truck. His cell keeps cutting in and out. I can hardly hear him.

"The highway's jammed. We're barely crawling. I'm just sitting here with my trailer full of calves. It'll be ages before I can get back. You're going to have to go."

I try to push back my panic. I try to think.

"Can you hear me?" he says.

"Yes, I hear you."

"You can't wait any longer. You've only got the one road out of there. You gotta go now."

"We're moving," I say.

~

7:20 A.M.

"Jane?" I call out.

The house is quiet. I go through the living room to the bottom of the stairs.

"Jane! Where are you?"

I wait.

"Jane!"

I don't have time for her stupid games right now. I charge up the stairs, two at a time. I shove open her bedroom door. "Could you at least answer me when—"

She's not there.

There's a heap of shopping bags, spilling over with her stuff, on the floor by her bunk bed. Hoodie's draped over top. I grab it. Not having Hoodie, wherever we end up tonight, is unthinkable.

I'm more pissed off than worried. I check my room and Margaret's. Back downstairs, through the living room, out to the verandah. Calling her name. Back into the kitchen and mudroom and then outside.

Now my heart's racing. Where the hell is she?

Wayne's dragging hoses.

"Wayne!" I shout. "I can't find Jane."

# CHAPTER FIFTY-ONE

"She was asking me for duct tape," says Wayne.

"Duct tape? When?"

"A while ago."

"I thought she was in her room packing. And what do you mean 'duct tape'? What did she want duct tape for?"

"I don't know. She went into the laundry room."

It's over an hour since I've actually seen Jane. I run back inside, fling open the laundry room door. I stand still.

Two laundry baskets of dirty clothes, a pile of Jane's sheets ready for folding, Wayne's plaid shirts on the drying rack, the kitty litter tray that's still in the corner of the room…something's missing.

On the counter, the roll of duct tape, scissors, and scattered pieces of twisted tape. Mr. Boney's house is gone.

~

"Jane's gone to the old house to get Mr. Boney," I say. "Shit."

"You don't know that," says Wayne.

"Yes, I do."

Wayne's still gripping the end of the hose. He's starting to wheeze.

"I'm going to go get her," I say. "You go inside. And don't you get all stubborn on me. I mean it. You can't keep breathing this smoke. Go inside."

I realize that I'm still holding onto Hoodie. My eyes pool.

"Drive down in the truck," says Wayne. "It'll be faster."

~

The truck bounces over the old tractor road. The front tires dive into a hidden dip and I lurch forward. I grip the steering wheel tighter. A voice in my head is chanting over and over, *Just go! Just go! Just go!*

I glance over at Hoodie, laying on the seat beside me. I fight back tears again because I really have no idea where Jane is. I can see far enough ahead through the smoke to keep myself on the road. The slender branches of the aspens whip against the windshield. Rocks have worked their way up to the surface. I wince every time I hit one.

There's a loud clang and then *BANG-BANG-BANG* underneath the truck. I know that sound. The exhaust pipe's come loose and is dragging over the ground, hitting rocks.

I bite down on my lip. It doesn't matter. Just keep going.

The dragging noise is louder and louder. I go over a little rise and I'm looking down at the old house. Beyond it, the marsh is yellow and stagnant. I spot Mr. Boney's house lying in the long grass. Then I see Jane, standing in front of the sagging door frame, clutching a bundle of orange fur.

She's looking up.

I drive almost to the house, leave the truck in park, motor running, and jump out. "Get in the truck now, Jane!"

"No," she says.

"What?"

"No."

I want to shake her. "Get in the truck!"

"No. Look!" She pulls Mr. Boney against her chest with one hand. He's limp, dirty, hanging like a sack. I'm sure he's dead. She points with her other hand at the roof. "Look!"

I see nothing, just the old mossy shingles riddled with holes, and then there's a slight movement. Something very tiny, orange, gripping tightly to a shingle.

"Mr. Boney was up there, too, but he jumped down when he saw me," says Jane. "Do you see him, Rachel? It's Mr. Boney's kitten!"

~

Jane and I are standing in the upstairs room that's next to our secret room. It has a small window looking over the marsh. No glass. Through a gaping hole in the low ceiling, you can see the black edges of shingles and above them, gray smoke.

Before I can stop her, Jane, still clutching Mr. Boney, climbs up onto the windowsill and sticks her head out. "See, Mr. Boney? Your baby is right there. Come on, baby."

God. I grab her and pull her back. "Do you want to break your neck?"

She's still, her cheek pressed against Mr. Boney, her eyes fixed on me. "Please, Rachel," she says. "You gotta save him. He's gonna die."

I lean out the window as far as I can. He's right there, almost close enough to touch. I stretch out my hand. "C'mon, little guy. You can do it."

Milky blue eyes in a dirty orange face. I'm not sure how clearly he can see me. Or if he can see me at all.

"C'mon," I say.

"What's he doing?" says Jane.

The kitten scrunches into a ball. This is probably the stupidest thing I have ever done in my entire life, but it's the only thing I can think of. Because the only person more stubborn than Wayne is Jane, and Jane will not leave without that kitten.

I swing one foot over the windowsill and feel around until I find a spot that seems solid. I swing the other foot over, and I'm on the roof. I plop right down with my back pressed against the wall below the window.

Now what?

I'm holding on for dear life to a rotten roof full of holes that I just know is going to cave in any second. What the hell am I doing out here?

I don't dare try to stand up. I scootch toward the kitten on my butt. My jeans catch on an old nail on the edge of a shingle, and I come to a dead stop. Carefully, I free my jeans and edge almost within touching distance. I reach out my hand. "Come on."

I hold my breath. I think he hears my voice. He's moving toward me, just barely, but enough. I scoop him up and slip him into the front of my T-shirt. He weighs nothing. His tiny claws clutch my skin, like pinpricks. He's such a baby. I wiggle my way back to the window. "I got him!"

"Oh my God," says Jane.

I pass him carefully through the window into her hands, then climb through and lower myself to the floor. A long scrape along the inside of my left arm is oozing blood. Where did that come from? My legs are shaking.

The kitten tries to burrow into Mr. Boney's ragged, matted fur. Maybe he's searching for a teat. He must be starving. For a second, Mr. Boney's eyes open into green slits, then they drop shut.

"Let's go!" I say.

We clatter down the stairs, me behind Jane.

When we get outside, I slam to a stop. Brown smoke is spewing out from under the truck. A gust of hot air blows in our face. Wind, the same wind that's coming all the way from Slack Lake, the wind that's chasing the fire up to our plateau. Smoke billows up, swirling. A ribbon of fire shoots out from under the back of the truck, streaks through the grass.

My heart pounds. "Fuck!"

Flames burst into the air, knee-high, a sheet of fire between us and the truck. Mr. Boney's cardboard house catches fire. The wind picks it up, a burning ball, and tosses it a few feet.

There's an entire marsh of water beside us and we have nothing, not even a bucket. More gusts of wind sweep the fire across the brittle grass toward the ancient logs of the house. Toward us.

Jane screams.

I grab her arm. "Run!"

# CHAPTER FIFTY-TWO

The hayfield is faster than the road. We climb up the slope. Jane's cradling the tiny kitten in her hands, sobbing. I hold Mr. Boney, trying not to squeeze him too tightly. He's so frail. Through my T-shirt, I feel his heart tapping faintly. The ground's uneven with dips and mounds of dirt left by gophers. Rough grass slaps against our bare legs. We're both coughing, tears streaming down our cheeks.

I look back once. A funnel of jet-black smoke is shooting into the sky. What's that? Then I know. Burning rubber from tires.

Shit, shit, shit.

This is how it happens. A dropped cigarette, a campfire left to burn, two kids trying to roast marshmallows. A hot exhaust pipe dragging on the ground.

Jane trips, cries out, and tumbles onto her knees. She's smashed into an old, half-rotten hayrack, hidden by the long grass. I help her up. Blood gushes from her left shin.

"I thought I could catch Mr. Boney." Jane's trying to speak through little sobs. "I was gonna carry him in his house...so he wouldn't run away again...."

"It's okay," I say. "I've got him. Keep going."

"I've got a name for the kitten," she gasps, stumbling along beside me. "Cinders."

~

Wayne's standing by the fence. Waiting.

"You found her." He pulls Jane against his chest. "Don't you pull a stunt like that again, young lady."

"Don't squish Cinders!" says Jane.

Wayne looks at the kitten, then at Mr. Boney, and finally at me. "Where's the truck?" he says.

"It's on fire," says Jane.

"The exhaust pipe," I say. "That must be what happened. It fell down. It was scraping on rocks. It must have got so hot it set the grass on fire—" My throat closes. I can't choke even one more word out.

Wayne gazes out toward the marsh, but it's hidden now in smoke. We can't see past the corral fence. What is he thinking? I can't tell. He says, "Take Mr. Boney and his kitten in the house, Jane. Wash the blood off your leg off and get some Band-Aids."

When she's gone, he says, "We'll be okay. I think I can hook up the old well to the pump house. That'll give us a lot more water."

We have the new well that was dug twenty years ago and the old well, which is never used anymore. He's talking about wells and his lungs are probably turning into soot because he's breathing in too much smoke. He's not thinking straight. Everything, *everything* is depending on me.

"You were supposed to be inside," I say. "I told you—"

"You can give me a hand in a minute. There's a broken sprinkler in the shed. I can probably do something to rig that up, too."

"Go inside, Wayne. And could you stop talking about sprinklers? I don't give a *shit* about sprinklers. We don't have a truck! Do you even know what that means?"

"We'll put a sprinkler on the roof." He turns, starts trudging toward the pump house.

"We have no way out of here!" I shout.

# CHAPTER FIFTY-THREE

"Sit in this chair," I say. "And don't move."

I give Wayne a glass of water and take his blood pressure. 170 over 106. I check the card on the fridge.

*Very worrying.*

~

I call Leslie. She answers on the third ring. "Corporal Leslie Wagner. RCMP."

"It's me. Rachel."

I talk too fast and I'm not making any sense. She tells me to slow down, start again. She listens, then says calmly, "The highway's clogged so I can't get a car in. Can Wayne walk as far as the lakeshore?"

"He walks on the driveway, but he finds it really hard. The lake is so much farther. And his blood pressure's terrible. I don't know if he can make it."

"I want you to try. I'll send a speedboat."

~

We're ready. Leashes for Bella and Lucy. Mr. Boney and Cinders safe inside Lucy's puppy crate.

I've packed apples and bananas and cookies in Jane's pink backpack. My phone, a couple pairs of shorts and T-shirts for me and Jane, two of Wayne's plaid shirts, a pair of his long pants, his medication all go into my backpack. We have no Grab and Go bags. They're in the truck. I won't let my mind go any further than that.

What else?

"I have to go and get something from my room," says Jane. She never did put Band-Aids on her leg. There's a river of dried blood from her shin into her running shoe.

"Two minutes," I say. "And just your room. Nowhere else."

Jane races upstairs. Wayne's leaning against the kitchen sink, sucking down another big glass of water.

He says, "You girls go. I'm staying here."

Whatever made me think that Wayne would walk away from four generations of Bird history?

"Don't do this to me." I try to keep my voice even. "Not now. You can't do this to me, Wayne."

Wayne puts his empty glass in the sink. He turns and looks at me. "Someone needs to be here to move the sprinklers," he says. "I'll be fine."

"You'll be fine? How can you even say that?"

"I think I can save the house."

"Are you out of your mind? You want to save the house? The *house*? What about you? You don't think you're more important than a house?"

Wayne's face closes in.

"Jane and I need you alive. Not dead."

"Listen—" he says.

"No. *You* listen to me." I am so angry I can hardly talk. But I'm not finished. "When Mom died, it was the worst thing that ever happened to us." I stop, swallow past the lump that's squeezing my throat. "And then we came here, and now we have a family. It's not about a house. It's about our family. You and Margaret and Uncle Rob and me and Jane. We're a family. And you're part of it, Wayne. Don't you dare risk that. Do you hear me? Don't you dare."

Wayne is silent. He goes into the mudroom, and I'm thinking that he hasn't heard one word, that he's going back outside to his stupid sprinklers. But then he's back, holding his black cowboy hat.

"Time to get outta here," he says.

When I can trust my voice again, I say, "Good. Because if something happened to you, who would call me girlie?"

~

Jane's in the kitchen doorway. "I can't find Hoodie," she says.

I'm going to carry the crate and my backpack, Jane will carry her backpack and hold onto Lucy's leash to keep her from running off. I can trust Bella. She'd never leave Wayne. Both dogs are twining anxiously under our feet. There's been no sound at all from the cats inside the crate.

Wayne has his canes. He has to put all his energy into walking.

I forgot water bottles. I fill three, one for each of us. A fourth bottle and a small bowl for the dogs. Two water bottles in my backpack, two in Jane's. She's hovering at my elbow.

"Hoodie's in the truck," I say. "I've told you three times. That's all I know. I'm sorry."

"You shouldn't have taken it. It's mine."

"I know. And I'm sorry."

Jane's lower lip is wobbling. She's trying really hard not to cry. "What do you think happened to it?"

"I don't know! Stop asking me!"

"O-*kay*."

I know I'm being mean. But I don't know what's happened to any of our things in the truck. I can't let my head go there right now.

There are two ways to get to the lake, through a field or the trail in the woods. "We'll take the trail," I say. "That's the easiest way for you, Wayne."

"Lock the door," he says. "I don't want looters in here."

We step outside.

The smoke has lifted again. It's playing a game with us. In the distance, the sky over the marsh and the old house is crimson.

# CHAPTER FIFTY-FOUR

Wayne knows every inch of these woods. Every inch of all the woods on our ranch. Every time you walk on a trail anywhere on this ranch, you know that Wayne or my great-grandfather or my great-great-grandfather made that trail.

Margaret told me that every spring, Wayne used to go out with his chainsaw and clear the trails of fallen trees and huge branches left from winter storms. He can't do that anymore, but his presence on the ranch is everywhere. The clearing where he used to cut firewood; the meadow where he shot an injured moose, putting it out of its misery; the place where Bella treed a bear. I bet he can tell you every pine tree that the pine beetles killed and all the places where the new pine trees are growing.

He's walking slowly now. "Look at everything, girls." His voice is matter-of-fact. "You have to save all this in your mind so you'll have it if you need to remember."

We're leaving and we have no idea what we'll come back to. I can't save it all. There's too much. This is what I'll try to save:

Me and Jane and the dogs, racing down this trail in our bathing suits and flip-flops, splashing straight into the lake.

Margaret in her polka-dot bathing suit and Wayne's old running shoes that are too big, but she won't wade into the lake without them.

Walking holding hands with Cody, our bare feet hopping on the hard ground because we were trying to prove we were tough. It was November, a dust of snow, way too cold to be barefoot, and it was Cody's idea. It was so ridiculous and so fun.

"I'm saving all the animals," says Jane.

"Good," says Wayne.

"Can you save two things?"

"Why not?"

"Then I'm saving all the trees, too."

I'll save the time when Jane and I found the diving rock. When I paddled my own canoe for the first time. When Amber and I rode Magic and Champion right down this trail to the lake and went swimming with them. When a few feet of new snow buried the trail, and Carlee and I made tracks in our skis right onto the frozen lake.

Wayne stumbles and I grab his arm. He feels so frail through his plaid shirt. I slide my hand into his and he grips tightly.

"Stop for a minute so you can catch your breath." I help ease him onto a log at the side of the trail. He's fighting to get air.

"It's so goddamn hot," he mutters. He takes off his cowboy hat and wipes his hand across his brow.

It's not hot. Not at all like last week's heat. I put my backpack on the ground and take out a water bottle. "Drink this."

He sips slowly, then gives me the bottle back and rests his elbows on his knees, staring at the ground. Bella pokes her nose into his hand and whines. He rubs her head.

"Are you sick, Papa?" says Jane.

"Just a bit tired, Jane-O."

Then the distant roar of a motorboat breaks the silence of the woods.

"Here comes the cavalry," he says. "You girls get down there so they'll know we're here. Tell them I'm coming."

I look Wayne straight in the eyes. "Leave you by yourself so you can cook up some new scheme? Not a chance."

Jane runs ahead with Lucy. Wayne and Bella and I follow the winding trail, the crate banging against my leg. Wayne can barely control his canes, stabbing the ground weakly or flailing them sideways. We take it step by step, pausing every few minutes so he can rest. Finally, through trees, we glimpse a strip of flat, dull water. I help him out to the grassy shore where he sinks onto a log.

The smoke is patchy, coming and going. At first, all we can see across the lake is a long, gray smudge that's the opposite shore. Then the smoke thins. Orange flames are climbing up from behind the ridge.

"That's High Valley Ranch," says Wayne.

I can't tear my eyes away. The flames are alive, licking the sky.

Jane's standing at the edge of the water waving both arms. Lucy and Bella are barking. A white speedboat appears through the haze, motoring in slowly. A man in an RCMP uniform climbs onto the bow, holding a rope. He springs onto the bank. "Am I glad to see you folks," he says. "Joe Porter."

Wayne uses my shoulder to stand up. He steps forward and reaches out his hand. "I'm the owner of this ranch. Wayne Bird."

# CHAPTER FIFTY-FIVE

Leslie's behind the steering wheel in the front of the boat. "Well done, guys," she calls out. "We're going to get you out of here. Jane, you think you can wade out by yourself?"

"Yes!" says Jane.

"Okay, everybody. We're not going to worry about shoes and clothes getting wet. Let's go!"

Jane splashes to the boat. Leslie steps into the back and reaches over, grabs her backpack, and helps her scramble onboard.

Joe takes Wayne's arm, and they wade into the lake. The bottom is soft with mud and it looks like Wayne's having trouble moving his feet. "One step at a time," says Joe. "No rush, Wayne. We can do this."

One step at a time.

I tell the dogs to come, and I follow with the crate.

"Rachel, they're not coming!" shouts Jane.

I turn around. Lucy's charging up and down the bank, barking her head off, and Bella's standing in the shallow water, whining.

"Lucy!" shouts Jane again. "Bella! Come!"

"Lucy! Bella!" I yell.

Bella starts to swim and Lucy plunges in after her. Bella swims steadily to the boat, snorting water out her nose. Lucy circles around my legs, almost knocking me over, and I have to shove her away. Leslie lowers a small metal ladder over the side. Wayne climbs up slowly, grunting. He's in. He slides onto a bench.

Joe waits for me. He takes the crate and hands it up to Leslie. I pass her my backpack. Together, from the water, we wrestle the slippery dogs into the boat. I climb in next and then Joe.

Jane and I sit on the bench opposite Wayne. The dogs are in the back, the crate in front of me. Joe hands out life jackets. He helps Jane and I buckle up ours and then Wayne's. Then he sits down beside Wayne.

"Everyone ready?" says Leslie.

"I'm good," says Wayne.

"Ready!" I say.

"Let's do this." She circles the boat and we take off, the bow tipping up in the air, carving two long wakes behind us.

*We're safe. We're going.*

Over the roar of the boat engine, we hear a humming noise, high up.

"Hey!" says Jane, tilting her head back.

A helicopter is hovering, quite far to our right. A long cable with a huge bucket on the end hangs from the helicopter's belly, straight down to the lake. The bucket sinks into the water, then it's out again, swinging, and the helicopter spins away.

"They've been scooping water from different lakes all morning," says Joe. "Every time they get a window in the smoke. They're dumping fire retardant on the fire, too. We're going to beat this."

He leans toward Wayne. "How are you feeling?"

Wayne's face is pale and clammy. But he gives a thumbs-up. Joe reaches for his wrist. He holds it, looking at his watch, frowning. Then he takes out his phone.

It's almost impossible to hear what he's saying over the boat engine, but I catch this much: *Cardiac risk...an ambulance.*

~

An ambulance and a cop car meet us at the end of the lake.

Leslie goes with Wayne in the ambulance, we say goodbye to Joe, and then Jane and I and the dogs and the cats crowd into the cop car with Constable Mowatt. I recognize him from the meeting at our hall. He was the one who tried to talk to the woman with the chickens. Jane's in the front, I'm between Bella and Lucy in the back, the crate on the floor.

The dogs are making wet patches on the seat and my runners are leaking water, but I don't think Constable Mowatt cares. Jane's eating the cookies from her backpack and telling him all about Mr. Boney and Cinders. He's listening and asking questions.

Siren blaring and red lights flashing, we fly to Hundred Mile on the wrong side of the highway. The right lane is a solid line of cars and trucks heading into town. Our lane's deserted. Faces in the crawling cars, pressed against side windows, watch us go by.

Our first ride in a cop car.

I lean forward. "Please take us to the hospital."

Constable Mowatt glances in the rearview mirror. "It'd be better to drop you off at the community center. Leslie says there's people there waiting for you. We can get you registered."

"The hospital," I say.

"Okay. The hospital it is. And don't you worry, your grandpa will be okay."

Jane bursts into tears.

~

Pets aren't allowed inside the hospital. Jane, Lucy, Bella, the cats, and I wait outside in a little seating area. A nurse has promised to come and tell us as soon as she has news. Two people are sitting in the sun, a man in a wheelchair and a woman with gray hair, holding his hand. She looks exhausted.

I text Martin and Jesse.

We're here. We're at the hospital with Wayne.

Then Cody.

We're at the hospital. Please come.

Next, I call Margaret. She doesn't pick up. She never remembers to charge her phone. I try the number for Hummingbird Haven. A woman tells me that Margaret's been so worried, that she'll find her and give her the message right away.

Jane's sitting on a bench. She's taken her wet runners off and she's barefoot, swinging her legs. I'm barefoot, too, pacing back and forth. Lucy edges toward the woman and the man in the wheelchair. The woman smiles at Jane.

"We rode in a boat and a police car," says Jane.

"Wow," says the woman. Lucy thumps her tail, and she asks, "Can I pet your dog?"

"Yes," says Jane.

Lucy wriggles with joy. She never gets to leave the ranch. This is her great adventure. Bella's lying on the pavement with her chin on her front paws, waiting for Wayne to come back.

"Lucy is my dog," says Jane. "Bella is Papa's. I have two cats, too. Do you want to see them?"

"Oh, I do," says the woman.

Jane gets down on her hands and knees and peers through the wire door of the crate. She releases the latch and opens the door. She reaches her hand in.

Then she says, "Rachel!"

I crouch down beside her.

Somewhere between our kitchen and the hospital parking lot, Mr. Boney died.

# CHAPTER FIFTY-SIX

The community center is a ten-minute walk from the hospital. Cody gets here in five. I think he ran all the way.

He hugs me so hard. We both start talking at once.

"I'm sorry," I say. "We should've left—"

"We should've helped—"

I pour out a garbled story of the old house, climbing on the roof to get the cat, the truck on fire—everything. "And then Wayne wouldn't go, and I was freaking out and—"

"It's okay," says Cody. "You're safe, Rachel. You're here. And don't ever say you're sorry for what happened. You were amazing."

"And me, too?" says Jane. Her face is streaked with tears. "Was I amazing, too?"

"You sure were," says Cody.

"Mr. Boney died," I say softly.

"Oh, shit," says Cody.

Martin's truck wheels into the parking lot. Cody stays with Jane, the dogs, and the cats. Without even being asked. Because that's how

Cody is. When I leave, he's crouched in front of the crate with Jane. I go into the hospital with Martin. He seems to know everyone who works here and we're fast-tracked into the emergency wing. We walk past a row of curtained cubicles. A man's groaning in one, shouting for a nurse. Wayne's at the very end.

He's on a bed, hooked up to oxygen, which is frightening, and his eyes are closed. But the nurse who's with us says, "He's doing fine. Just tuckered out. We're going to keep him for a while for observation. We're getting a bed ready in a ward."

My legs feel like they're going to collapse. We go to the nursing station where she brings up the list of Wayne's medications. I check to make sure everything's there.

There's nothing else I can do. Except one thing. On our way past, I stop and gently pull back Wayne's curtain. I don't want to wake him up. I just want to tell him we love him.

When we get back outside, my phone rings. It's Margaret.

~

The community center's packed with people. There are still people from Slack Lake, and now most of Aspen Lake is here, too. We've got a banner over the door. *Welcome Aspen Lake.* Everyone's milling around, hugging, talking, crying. Tables are set up at the door for registration. Other tables along the walls have boxes of donuts and muffins, cartons of juice and coffee urns.

I register us with a girl who I recognize from school. She's two years ahead of me, in Grade Twelve. She explains how everything works. Jane and I will be eating here and sleeping on cots in the elementary school gymnasium. I can imagine these cots. I won't sleep a wink.

Martin, Susan, Amber, and Cassie are going to their friends' place at Seventy Mile. Jesse has a brother in town, and they're all planning on staying with him. Kit and Lois are heading there now with Lucy and Bella. Everyone else is still hanging around here because this is where we want to be. Together.

For a few minutes, at the hospital, I felt so relieved, like it was finally over. But I know it's not. We're still in the middle of this. No one knows exactly where the fire is, what's going to happen next, if Aspen Lake will be another Kwantan. No one knows if we'll have anything to go home to. Or if we'll even go home.

I've left Jane in a quiet corner at the back of the room with the crate. She's sitting cross-legged on the floor, Cinders in her lap.

I squat down beside her. "How's he doing?"

"I don't know." She chews at her bottom lip. "He's not purring."

I look at the tiny ball of scruffy fur. "I don't think kittens that little know how to purr yet. Put him back inside with Mr. Boney, Jane. We'll take him to the vet."

~

Cody comes, too. He won't let go of my hand.

We crowd into the examining room with Jessica, the vet. I set the crate on the floor, open the door, and lift Mr. Boney out carefully. I'm shocked by how light he feels. Despite having had kittens, Mr. Boney will always be a *he*. He's mostly ribs and matted orange fur, not much different from when Jane first brought him home. I lay him down on a white mat on the metal table.

"Mr. Boney was Jane's cat," I say.

"He's a girl," whispers Jane. Her eyes are wide. I do that, too, when I'm trying to keep tears back.

Jessica gently palpitates Mr. Boney's tummy. "I think he had a very hard time being pregnant, Jane, and then he had a family to look after during a heat dome. But there might have been more than that going on. I can feel something here. Maybe a tumor."

"Oh," says Jane.

"Do you cremate cats?" I ask.

Jane knows all about ashes and cremation. And I don't know what else to do with him.

"Yes, we can do that," says Jessica.

"It's a good idea," says Cody.

"I guess it's okay," says Jane.

Jessica smiles. "Now, let me see the little one."

Jane kneels down and takes Cinders out of the crate. She holds him up, a ragged, filthy orange ball with half-shut eyes.

Jessica takes the kitten gently in her hands. "Let's take a look," she says. "Ah, a boy. He's a champion little fellow. I'd say about nine days old. His eyes have probably just opened, but he won't be seeing really well yet. Let's put him on the table so I can see him properly."

She examines his eyes and ears and puts a stethoscope on his tiny chest. "Nothing seriously wrong here. But I'd like you to leave him with me for a few days. I'll hook him up to an IV and give him some fluids and nutrients. He'll be as good as new."

"Would it be like staying in the hospital?" says Jane.

"Exactly like that."

"Wayne and Cinders can compare notes," says Cody.

"I promise we'll take good care of him," says Jessica. "What do you think, Jane?"

"Okay."

"You can come back and see him while you're here. Now you guys stay strong. We're all praying that you get back to Aspen Lake soon. The whole town's with you."

"Thank you," I say.

When we're back outside, Cody says, "We can put Mr. Boney's ashes somewhere really great. We could sprinkle them on the lake or in the garden or in the woods. Where was his favorite place, Jane?"

"The laundry room," she says.

# CHAPTER FIFTY-SEVEN

When we get back to the community center, people are crowding around a whiteboard that's updated when new information on the fire comes in. I'm feeling hot and slightly dizzy. I find a chair and sit. I'm trying to take it all in, but I'm totally drained. Cody keeps checking and reporting back. It's good and bad. They're hitting the fire hard, and it hasn't advanced in the last two hours. But stronger winds are forecasted. Acres burned: two hundred thousand.

Shanda from the library is trying to gather up little kids for a story time in the cloakroom area. Women start carrying out food from the kitchen at the back, huge pots of chili, bowls of salad, plastic bags of buns, paper plates, and plastic knives and forks. Harjit and her husband, Mr. Minhas, come through the front door with two huge lasagnas. I go over to help them.

We stack the boxes on the free end of a table, then Harjit and I hug. I fill them in on what's happened.

"I'll pop in to see Wayne," Harjit promises. They've met a few times. She calls him the salt of the earth.

More food come in the front door. More salads, platters of sandwiches. I don't think I'll ever feel like eating. I think back over everything that's happened since this morning, and the backs of my eyes burn. I could have done it so much better.

Why did we wait so long to go? We should have left when Martin and everyone left. We should have been ready. Jane would never have run away to the old house. Wayne could have been driven out, instead of half killing himself as he struggled to get to the lake.

Because we would have had the truck.

That's where I stop. I can't let myself think about the truck and the flames racing through the grass to the old house. I can't think about the crimson sky.

Maybe it's over for me now. There are so many people here who have taken charge. It's crazy to feel relieved when everything's still so awful, but I do. I don't have to do anything anymore. I don't have to look after anyone.

Well, there's still Jane. She and Cassie are racing around, weaving in and out of people. Jane's face is scarlet, and she's clutching a bright pink donut in each hand. Cassie has a chocolate donut and a paper cup sloshing over with juice.

"Sugar high," says Cody. "Have fun tonight."

Emma, Sarah, Tyson, and Dai come flying through the front door of the hall with pizza boxes.

"Rachel!" shrieks Emma. "Cody texted and said you were here!" She gives me an enormous hug. "God! We were petrified for you!"

Sarah holds up a box. "In here is the plainest pizza they make. Just sauce and half the cheese!"

Now I'm going to cry. Sarah smiles, and I smile back. She gives me an awkward one-hand-holding-the-pizza-box hug, but it feels great. This is the first time Sarah and I have ever hugged.

"Now we can relax finally," says Tyson. "Jesus. Everyone's been freaking out about you, Rach." But he and Dai are grinning.

My phone dings. A text from Carlee.

I'm coming as soon as I can get a ride!

We sit in a circle on the floor. I'm between Cody and Sarah. Everyone's talking high speed at the same time. Exchanging stories. Me too. I've had a sudden burst of energy. The way Cody tells it, our rescue from the lake by the RCMP boat, fire sweeping toward us, makes me some kind of hero.

It took a wildfire to make me realize that I belong. I think I've belonged for a long time. I just didn't know how to accept it.

# CHAPTER FIFTY-EIGHT

DAY 2 OF EVACUATION

The fire has stalled—it's not going forward, and it's not going away. The firefighting crews are exhausted. The first soldiers arrived in BC yesterday. Total acres burned: two hundred and thirty thousand.

Jane and I are allowed to visit Wayne for fifteen minutes. He looks pretty good, and he's dying to get out of there. He wants paper and a pen. He's going to write letters about what they should have done for the fire.

When we leave, we can hear him halfway down the hallway, shouting on the phone to Margaret. "It's a goddamn disgrace, and I'm—"

We visit Cinders. He burrows into Jane's arms, purring. I help Harjit for an hour at Wagonroad Books, shelving new stock, and we talk nonstop. A bunch of us go to see *Spiderman: No Way Home* at the movie theater. Is the title prophetic? I hope not. Cody and I hold hands in the dark and kiss a lot. Then I fall asleep and miss the second half.

The cot in the school gymnasium? I am seriously sleep-deprived.

Will this ever end?

As a last resort, I eat two chocolate donuts. Then I barf.

~

DAY 3 OF EVACUATION

At 2:30 in the afternoon, everyone's hanging around outside the community center, watching the sky. All of us from Slack Lake and Aspen Lake and people from Hundred Mile who have been here day and night. Strangers who have become friends.

At 3:15 pm, the first raindrops fall from the heavy gray clouds. One hour later than forecasted. Everyone cheers.

By 3:35, it's a deluge.

~

## *100 MILE FREE PRESS*

### RAIN BRINGS WELCOME RELIEF

Fifteen hundred people, evacuated from their homes in Slack Lake and Aspen Lake, have been allowed to return home. Due to two days of heavy rainfall, the Slack Lake fire is now ninety percent contained with fire barriers constructed on all flanks. The weather forecast for the One Hundred Mile House area calls for scattered showers and sun for the next ten days. Many people from both communities have expressed their gratitude for the welcome, the accommodation, and the support they received from the motels, local businesses, and private citizens in One Hundred Mile House.

~

It's five more days until we go home. Martin gives us a full report. The fire reached the edge of High Valley Ranch. No further. I stay at Cody's, and Jane stays with Cassie until Wayne's well enough to leave the hospital. The highways into the Cariboo reopen. We've rejoined the world. Susan goes to Vancouver to get Margaret.

# CHAPTER FIFTY-NINE

Jane's squeezed in between me and Wayne, craning forward. We're bouncing over the ruts in the old tractor road. It's drizzling and the windshield wipers of our rental jeep are making a scraping sound. The drizzle turns to a steady rain. *Swish, swish.* The wipers move smoothly now. The windshield steams up and I rub a circle with my hand.

I stop the jeep at the bottom of the road, shut it off. We sit for a minute, listening to the ticking motor. I've tried to prepare myself, but the shock is still enormous. Jane is very still.

There's almost nothing left of the old house. Just a pile of burnt, black logs in a sea of scorched grass, the chimney of the old woodstove sticking up, the only survivor. A wide swath of black grass ends at the murky marsh.

Our truck is tilted on its rims, the tires gone. All the windows are spiderwebs of cracked glass. The black paint is blistered and bubbly.

"The marsh stopped the fire," says Wayne. "We will be thankful for that."

We get out of the jeep. The air is thick with the smell of wet, burnt wood. My hair and the back of my T-shirt are instantly sopping and there's rain dripping on my cheeks. I stare at the black, charred wood, and I see a little boy skiing in one door and out the other. I see Mom, sneaking up the old staircase to the little room. I see Mr. Boney's dead kittens.

There's a dull ache across my forehead. I think about the ghost in the cream-colored rose dress. Where will she live now? And what happened to the bottle we hid under the floorboards?

Layers of history. Gone.

It's not rain on my face, it's tears.

Jane dissolves into sobs.

"Come here," says Wayne. He tucks one arm around Jane, the other around me, and the smell of burnt wood mingles with the smell of his wet, wool shirt.

"Someone told me once that a house was just a house," he says. "That family was more important. She was very smart. It's sad, and we'll miss the old house, but it was just a house. Life happens. To houses and to things and to people. And the Birds keep on going. Nothing will stop us."

He pokes the end of one of his canes into the burnt grass. "You get down on your knees, Jane. I can't anymore, but you can. You tell me what you find."

Jane kneels, pushes her hands into the grass. "Oh my God! Little pieces of grass, Papa! Green grass!"

I summon up my courage to walk over to the truck. In the back, there's a pile of charred cloth, melted, twisted picture frames, black sooty things that I can't identify. We'll have to go through it all. See if there's anything we can salvage.

All this time we worried about the Slack Lake fire. But it was this fire that got us at the end. The fire I started. My fire.

I try to peer through the cracked front-side window, but it's like looking through lace. I have to tug hard on the door, but it finally swings open. The inside of the truck is covered in a film of gray soot. Otherwise, it's eerily untouched.

On the front seat is Hoodie.

# CHAPTER SIXTY

Hoodie is washed and hanging on the clothesline, blowing gently in the breeze. It hasn't smelled like Mom for a long time. It doesn't smell like smoke anymore, either.

Hoodie smells like sun and fresh air.

~

"Don't you go thinking that you were responsible for that fire," says Wayne.

We're sitting at the kitchen table, drinking coffee. Talking about the last few days.

"It was me who told you to take the truck," he says. "It was a chain of events. And a goddamn accident. The heat, the fire, wind, Jane running away, dry grass, an old exhaust pipe."

"Which I busted when I picked Jane up at the bus and drove into a ditch."

"Ah. So that's what happened to it."

We sit quietly for a few minutes, each lost in our own thoughts.

"Don't forget, I banished Mr. Boney to the barn," says Wayne. "You could say that's where it all started. You can always go backward and find something that caused something else. But you do what you believe is the right thing to do at that moment. That's all anyone can do."

I think about life being a whole long line of things that happen, each one because of something else. All joined together, until one thing goes sideways and nothing's ever the same again.

"Don't feel guilty, Rachel," says Wayne. "About anything in your life. Guilt is a hell of a burden to carry around. You move on."

Better than anyone, my grandfather would know.

~

Martin drags the truck onto a flatbed trailer and brings it up to the house. Jane and I sort through the rubble in the back. We make two piles—try to clean or throw away.

Jane's duffel bag was buried underneath everything else. It's recognizable. Her face and hands are instantly black as she pulls it apart. She finds:

Her stuffed penguin, with one ear burned off.

Her stuffed rabbit. Inexplicably still pink.

Her marble game, the box scorched and the pieces of plastic inside twisted into weird shapes.

A pool of melted crayons stuck to a singed pajama top.

Arrows with pieces of burnt feathers. The bow is stringless, but otherwise okay.

Nate the Great did not survive.

We pull out a sack of dog food, the top crumbling into ashes. A deformed plastic water jug.

Scraps of burnt, blue cloth that used to be my duffel bag. My heart bangs when I realize that the square of melted black plastic is my laptop. I can't find anything that might have been my Kindle. A piece of burnt cord—all that's left of my blow-dryer?

As for the cardboard box with our papers, birth certificates, documents? Everything that proves that we're here? That we exist?

Not a trace.

Only three of Margaret's photos escaped the flames. I wipe the blackened glass with a rag. There's a photo of Uncle Jimmy with a Mickey Mouse lunch kit, a nerdy photo of Uncle Rob with a new bicycle, a photo of Mom in her turquoise prom dress. Mom with her red pigtails is gone forever.

More than anything else, I've been praying that the photos would be okay. Protected by their frames and the glass. That's how much I know about fire. Maybe not all the photos, but more than three. I remember Carlee saying that her Aunt Marnie didn't give a shit about her furniture or anything. Just her photo albums. Now I get what she meant. Everything else is just stuff. Margaret's photos weren't digital. They're not saved on a phone or in the cloud. They were the old-fashioned film photos. We can't get them back. Ever.

I walk away for a few minutes because this is just too hard. If only I had left the photos where they belonged, on the walls of Margaret's bedroom. I never even asked her what she wanted me to do. I just took them. I try to still the nausea rising up inside me.

"Look what I found!" Jane calls out. She holds up a black, charred rib.

"Great!" I say. But what I'm thinking is, how will I tell Margaret? What will I tell her?

~

Aura sends texts throughout the day. She's been watching the international news. Then, at 3:30 in the afternoon, she phones.

It's 1:30 a.m. in Bulgaria. She's outside in the dark with one bar on her phone, hunting for a better signal.

"Can you hear me?" she says.

"Sort of."

A pause. "Is that better?"

"Worse," I say. "I thought you were disconnecting from technology. Or something like that."

A thud.

"Are you okay, Aura?"

"Uh, yup," she says. "Tripped on some loose pavement. You can hear me?"

"Right now I can."

"Listen up. You make sure you give yourself all the time you need to grieve, Rachel. And tell Jane. And remember, grieving isn't just for people who have died. It's for things, too."

~

Uncle Rob's coming home. He's booked on a flight from Warsaw in two days. He's going to start piecing together our identity again.

"Don't worry," he says. "There's nothing I like better than a good fight with our Canadian bureaucracy."

# CHAPTER SIXTY-ONE

Amber, Carlee, and I ride into the back quarter of High Valley Ranch. This is as far as the fire got. We're on a hill, looking down on a huge, scorched-black hayfield, rimmed with the trunks of black, leafless trees.

"Shit," says Carlee. "I'm so sorry, Amber."

She's riding Dancer and staying overnight. She's desperate for some space from all her family. Dancer and Champion have been snorting most of the way. Amber thinks they can still smell smoke. Magic's quieter, but I can feel tension in his neck.

"It could have been way worse," says Amber. "It won't hurt the field. Just no hay from there this year. We got our other fields. That part of the forest. . . ." She shrugs. "It was pretty riding in there, but we didn't really use it for anything."

"The fire was so close," I say.

"Yeah. And if High Valley Ranch had burned up, your ranch probably would've, too."

"Jesus," says Carlee. Dancer's fidgeting, and she turns him in a circle. "It's still so hard to believe all this happened. We've been so lucky in Rocky Lake. So removed from everything."

"In the big picture, we're all lucky," says Amber.

I think of Starla's family from Kwantan, of all the people in Kwantan, of all the people who have lost homes in fires across BC this summer. Amber's right. We are lucky.

Magic starts pawing at the ground with his front hoof, something he never does. He's unhappy here. I rub his neck and take one last look at the burnt forest. I remember riding in there with Margaret and Amber and Jane last summer, when there were so many blue lupines that Jane said we were riding in the sky. That day, we saw our first doe with speckled twin fawns.

"Go back now?" says Amber.

"Yeah," I say.

I've seen what I needed to see. But I haven't finished grieving.

~

We've been waiting all afternoon. Susan texts that there's lots of traffic on the highway. They keep getting held up, but they're coming.

A banner, ten feet long, painted on the back of an old roll of wall-paper, is duct taped across the front of the house.

**WELCOME HOME MARGARET**

Putting it up was a communal effort with me and Cody on ladders and Jane and Cassie, paint splattered, calling out "It's still crooked! It has to go up more on that side! It's still *crooked*!"

It's been raining for two days but the clouds have broken apart. Everything is steaming under a blazing sun. Amber and Samantha are in the kitchen making sandwiches and salads. Cody, Jesse, Martin, and Wayne are on the verandah, talking about the fire. Cassie's dragging a crunched-up tinfoil ball tied to a piece of string for Cinders to chase.

Jane's our scout. She makes another quick trip to the driveway and screams, "They're here!"

We congregate at the front of the house. Susan's blasting the horn as her car appears around the final bend in the driveway. Margaret gets out first. She looks radiant. Jane springs into her arms, and Margaret smiles at me over Jane's head. I can't stop grinning.

"Well then, Margaret," says Wayne, stumping forward on his canes. "Well then, I held the fort while you were gone. You'll see for yourself. Everything is under control."

# CHAPTER SIXTY-TWO

We're on the verandah, and everyone's finally stopped talking and eating.

I stand up, a white envelope in my hand. "Listen up everyone. I have something very important to read."

I slide out a piece of paper.

*Dear Mr. Bird,*

*Thank you for your submission of Free Like a Bird. Your manuscript came across my desk on Tuesday, postmarked two weeks ago from Aspen Lake.*

*You may be surprised at such a quick response. Your title captivated my attention! Once I started reading, I was hooked.*

*We are a small publishing company always looking for exciting stories that celebrate the unique history of this country. Your story does exactly that.*

*We are very pleased to tell you that we are enclosing a draft contract for publication of your book.*

*We are extremely excited about the potential of your story and look forward very much to working with you.*

*Warm regards,*

*Gerald Painer*

*Northern Sky Book Publishers*

"You changed the title!" says Margaret. "You clever man!"

~

Jane shows Margaret Mr. Boney's urn of ashes, a small blue pot. It's on the shelf above the washing machine, between a box of Tide and a bottle of bleach.

~

Then Margaret and I slip away from everyone and go to the garden.

"I think I killed it," I say.

She laughs. "Let's blame it all on the heat dome. Besides, you can't really kill a garden. It will come to life again. You wait and see. That's the great thing about gardens."

~

Martin, Susan, Amber, and Cassie have left. Jesse and Samantha and Wayne are in the living room, talking. Margaret's gone upstairs to unpack her suitcase and soak in the bathtub. Cody and I stayed outside on the verandah. He's lounging in Uncle Jimmy's willow chair and I'm on the floor, cross-legged, leaning against his knees.

I'm watching Jane give Cinders rides in the hammock and, at the same time, letting my thoughts drift all over the place. Cody starts braiding my hair, and I close my eyes. It feels so good.

"Hey!" says Jane.

I glance over at her.

She rolls out of the hammock, lands in a crouch, and scoops up something in the grass. She marches over to us and stretches out her hand.

"I found the ring!"

# CHAPTER SIXTY-THREE

"It's a long story," I say.

But I'm not sure what story I'm talking about.

Hunting through the daisies in the hayfield with the metal detector? Or why I'm just not ready to wear Cody's ring? Either way, it's time to explain.

"Let's walk," I suggest.

We go down to the old house. I'm going to always call it the old house, even though it's not there anymore. Grass will grow over everything, but Wayne says charred wood takes a long time to decay. It will be there for years. I'm hanging onto that.

Jane and I have been here twice. Once I came alone, to grieve by myself. Each time, I let myself see a little more. Broken glass, a long, thick piece of black wood that I identified as a rafter, a mud swallow nest, surprisingly unbroken. We never found our bottle.

Cody's poking around, looking at everything. The wet charcoal smell still lingers. Today, I spot something new glinting in the sun. I pick it out of the debris. It's the lid from Mom's tin chocolate box. You can still make out the horses. Jane will love it.

"I always thought you and me could've renovated this one day and lived in it," says Cody. "With your ghost."

He remembers my ghost. He gives me his great smile.

I make a face. "Ha-ha."

Then I say, "I'm going to give you the ring back."

"Now that you know where it is."

"I'm sorry." I hesitate, searching for the words. "It's not true that I don't care about you and our relationship. I do. But a ring is just too much. It makes me feel that everything is going too fast." I frown. I have to get the next part right. "It's not just the ring. It's having sex, too. I don't want to do that again. I'm not ready."

"I get it," he says. "I should've asked you about the ring first. Not just gone and done it. And, well, we can wait. I'm totally okay with that."

I stare out at the marsh. All the greens and browns blur together. I don't want to cry. Not now.

"But we're not breaking up?" he says.

I don't even have to think about this part of the story.

I slip my hand into his. "Are you kidding me? No."

~

We're in my room and Cody's standing by my desk, looking at my Paris application. When he finishes, he says, "Wow."

His "wow" is a little flat.

"You and Carlee and Harjit know, but no one else. I think Margaret will be okay with it. I'm just praying Wayne doesn't go ballistic."

"Is it super expensive?"

"Yes. But I can apply for financial assistance. And I've got my money from Wagonroad Books. But it depends on what Margaret and Wayne say."

"They'll have to let you go," he says.

"Why?" I ask.

"Because it's a great opportunity for you. Personally, I can't think of anything worse to do."

We both laugh."

"You mean it?" I say. "You really think so?"

"Yeah. I don't want you to go, but you should do it."

"And I'll miss you every single day."

"You better."

He pulls me toward him. "Just don't meet some French dude."

~

Everyone's gone now. Margaret and I are in her bedroom with all the empty picture hooks on the walls. I've been dreading this.

"I am so sorry." It feels like I'm saying that a lot these days, but each time I really mean it.

She puts her arm around my shoulder and squeezes. "In the middle of all the confusion, looking after Wayne and Jane, and I know what that's like, packing everything up, everyone panicking, you took the time to think about me," she says. "That's pretty amazing, Rachel."

My eyes prickle. You do what you think is right at the moment, and you move on. I guess that's what Wayne meant.

"And we haven't lost everything," she says. "I've got a shoebox of photos that need sorting. We'll pick some good ones out. And we'll get new photos. Of you and Jane and all your friends and our dogs and our cats. That doesn't mean we'll forget. We'll never forget. Okay?"

"Okay."

Of course, that's exactly what Margaret would say. Why was I so worried? She's resilient. She has to be. She's been married to a Bird for a very long time.

"Margaret?" I say. "I was wondering if you could help me with something."

~

I bring my application form back to her room. We close the door and sit on her bed. Margaret reads all the pages slowly.

"It looks interesting," she says.

Noncommittal? No, more promising than that.

"What do you think Wayne will say?"

"Don't worry about Wayne. I'll talk to him."

I let my breath out. This could really happen.

"I've answered all the questions," I say quickly. "Except the last one. 'What are four words that best describe you?' It's so hard to do that without sounding conceited. And I think it's really important to be honest."

"Yes, it is," says Margaret. "Have you thought of anything yet?"

I sigh. "Self-absorbed. That came from Carlee. Hot-tempered. That's what Cody always thinks."

Margaret looks like she's trying not to laugh. "Self-absorbed, hot-tempered. What's the third one?"

"Insecure," I say. "That's my contribution. That's as far as I got."

Now she does laugh. "Don't send it in yet."

We go to the kitchen and make tea and talk about almost everything that happened. (I'm saving the pregnancy scare for one of our middle-of-the-night talks.) It's been such a crazy, terrifying, weird time. But we made it.

I show Margaret my tattoo. “I’m going to need some time to get used to that,” she says. “So, Rachel. One more year of high school over. How’d everything go at the end?”

“Good.”

It does feel good. I think about Amber’s free advice. *Be unique.* I want to be unique, and I want to fit in, too. I know I can do both.

Margaret comes up with two new words to describe me.

Brave.

Loving.

For the third word, we use Wayne’s.

Smart.

One word to go.

~

I call Cody.

“Brave, loving, and smart,” I say. “You get to pick the fourth word.”

“Oh boy,” he says. “This is going to be fun.”

“Be nice. No insults.”

“I’m always nice.”

I can think of a lot of words to describe Cody. Most of them good. But I’ll save that for later.

“I got it,” he says. “Hot.”

# CHAPTER SIXTY-FOUR

We're spinning a giant spiderweb in Jane's bedroom. Jane, Cody, Cinders, and me. Margaret donated a basketful of yarn left over from sweaters, socks, and scarves. Pink, purple, green, turquoise balls.

It's Cody's idea.

"What do we do?" asks Jane.

"Watch me," he says.

No rules for this. Cody leaps around the room, hooking green yarn onto the door handle, the end of the curtain rod, the knob on the top dresser drawer. He looks so silly I burst out laughing. Jane dives in instantly. Up high—the ceiling lamp. Just above the floor—the bottom rung on the bunk bed ladder.

I'm in, too. We crisscross back and forth, ducking under each other, whooping and hollering.

We're a spiderweb factory.

When we've used up almost all the yarn, the room is a kaleidoscope of colors and we're crouched on our knees, trapped like flies in the middle.

"The problem is," says Cody, "making the spiderweb is way more fun than taking it apart."

"And I'm starving," says Jane. Cinders has spun himself into a pile of pink yarn and she's untangling him.

"It's not helpful to talk about food when you're stuck in a spiderweb," I say.

"Poutine," she says.

"Cherry Coke," says Cody.

"Apples," I say. "Margaret can put your supper on a tray and slide it across the floor, Jane. We'll figure out your breakfast later."

"Does that mean I get to sleep in the spiderweb?" says Jane.

I have visions of untangling her every morning. "Well. . . ."

"Please, please, please."

Footsteps thud on the stairs. One slow, heavy step after the other. We're all staring at the door when Wayne flings it open. He hasn't been up here since Jane and I moved in.

"What the hell is going on?" he thunders. "I'm trying to write. It sounds like a goddamn herd of elephants up here."

Jane grabs a stray ball of purple yarn and flings it at him.

"You listen to me, girlie," he roars.

"Papa called me girlie!" she says. "Rachel, Papa called me girlie!"

Jane's growing up. And she's growing up here.

I'm growing up here, too. How perfect is that?

# AFTERWORD

## BRITISH COLUMBIA BURNS

With the exception of One Hundred Mile House, the communities in this story are fictional.

However, the story was inspired by real events. Residents of British Columbia will never forget the summer of 2021. From June 25 to July 1, the western heat dome was the deadliest weather crisis ever recorded in Canada, with 661 heat-related deaths. On June 28, Canada's highest ever temperature of 49.6 degrees Celsius was recorded in the small interior town of Lytton. The next day, a wildfire incinerated almost the entire town.

It is predicted that due to climate change, the frequency, severity, and duration of extreme heat domes and wildfire seasons will increase. The year 2023 was another crisis year in British Columbia, with a record number of acres and buildings destroyed by wildfires.

BC keeps burning!

# ACKNOWLEDGMENTS

A huge thank-you to everyone who helped me in so many incredible ways to tell Rachel's story. The team at Second Story Press is always amazing. Jordan Ryder and Heather Tekavec edited the book with insight, meticulous attention to detail, and such enthusiasm! It was exciting to see the story evolve and become so much stronger with their input. I would like to thank Wendy Marshall, our local bird expert, who shared her keen observations of nature and helped me define the setting. Thank you also to my dear friend Nikki James for her medical expertise. A special thank-you to Harjit Minhas who lent me her name! I have fond memories of enjoying her delicious kheer and other goodies at her home in northern BC many years ago! My family is always a huge support. My sister, Janet, tirelessly reads every draft, contributing enormously to the final story. My husband, Larry, provides invaluable technological support and makes it possible for me to have the time to write. My daughter, Meghan, inspires me!

# ABOUT THE AUTHOR

**Becky Citra** is a former teacher and the author of twenty books for children. She lives part of the year on Saltspring Island and part of the year on a ranch in Bridge Lake, British Columbia. Becky enjoys hiking, kayaking, snowshoeing, and gardening. She brings her knowledge of the outdoors into her books, often writing about ranch life and the wilderness.